Lost Child

(Volume One)

Anguish in the Nantahala

by Gene Skellig

"Flea Circus" is a registered trade mark.

ISBN-13:   978-0-9878645-0-5

DEDICATION

This book is dedicated to my four children, to my future grandchildren, and to all the children whose future we sacrifice each and every day. If major decisions were in their hands, I doubt they would squander the air, water and life of our planet. After all, they are going to need it.

ACKNOWLEDGEMENTS

Thanks go to a supportive family and friends, a dedicated "Teditor" and a talented cover artist. A special thinks to Ron, who read through early versions of the *Lost Child* story and provided valuable feedback. Without their help and encouragement this project could not have been undertaken.

DISCLAIMER

The characters and events portrayed in this book are fictitious. Any resemblance to real world events or persons living or dead is purely coincidental or used fictitiously.

CONTENTS

1. FUTILITY   1
2. THE TALK   19
3. ROAD TRIP   37
4. EXPERT WITNESS   45
5. NANTAHALA GORGE   65
6. ANTICIPATION   75
7. CALM DOWN   87
8. SEARCHING   117
9. BEHAVIOR   127
10. B.S.   143
11. LIFE WITHOUT SUNSHINE   151
12. PRESCRIPTION   161
13. FRANKLIN   173
14. RESTRAINT   189
15. COUCH   215
16. NICE GRANNY   227
17. CABIN   241
18. DELIVERANCE   251
19. END TO ANGUISH   263
ABOUT THE AUTHOR   268

1

FUTILITY

With sweat dripping from his brow in the close humidity of the cave, Ed jammed a second wedge into a hole in the face of the rock. At just about eye level, he was working on a pesky, lumpy protrusion about the size of a sack of potatoes. Ed hoped to cleave it from the wall with just the three holes he had drilled with the Pionjar, because that's all there would ever be.

The old gas-powered drill had broken down yet again. The used Pionjar had cost them next to nothing, but represented considerable hours of tinkering and maintenance. It also symbolized Ed's dream that he and Clay would find something valuable in the old mine. The one-man drill-rig now stood uselessly by his feet, stuck in a test hole in the floor of the mine. Ed emitted a heavy sigh, acknowledging the ominous hint of things to come.

He had drilled three good holes in the rock before the machine had crapped out, so he finished the task. He inserted a double-beveled cold chisel and a tapered wedge into the last of the holes, like he had done in the first two, and struck the assembly with a heavy hammer. With the rock under considerable tension, the sudden sharp blow was enough to trigger a crack passing through each of the three holes. With a second blow, the chunk of rock fell to the floor of the cave.

The splash of mud that flew up into Ed's face would have hit his eyes if they weren't shielded by the plastic safety goggles. Even in dim light, the fresh, clean side of the rock stood out in contrast to the darkly stained color of the other surfaces of the large chunk. Ed moved over to the utility stand and tilted the bright lights downward, illuminating the rock. Taking his goggles off, he bent down and looked closely.

At first he felt a bit of excitement when he thought he saw some indicator minerals, but when he examined it through his magnifying glass, it was just another piece of unaltered granite.

Ed took a deep breath and let it out very slowly. He then trudged through the tunnel to the improvised lab the two men had set up on a wooden table.

"Anything?" Ed asked, hoping Clay was having more luck.

"Nope. Nada. Just another *rock*. You get that pimple off the wall?"

"Yeah. Nothing there." Ed said, exasperated.

Hearing the defeated tone in Ed's voice, Clay looked up from the microscope he had been looking through at the improvised sample-lab they had set up on an old table.

"You finally ready to accept reality?"

"Yeah. I give up. This has been a complete waste of time."

"That's what I've been saying. There's something we're not getting here, Ed," said Clay.

The two men had worked hard for the last week. First they had some trouble getting the three-inch pump working, to draw the water out of the abandoned mine. After two days of continuous pumping, the mine was finally theirs to explore.

After taking a full day to explore and map out the tunnels, they finally knew what they had to work with.

The abandoned mine was surprisingly extensive. It had a six hundred foot long ramp, sloping down under the hill, with a few branches veering to the left or right along the way, and a thirty-foot ventilation shaft near the deepest end.

After the mapping, they moved on to the sampling operation. The goal, of course, was to find out what the long forgotten mine had once produced. They found the mine almost by tragedy.

During one of their bow-hunting trips, Clay had come close to breaking his fool neck when he nearly did a backward swan-dive into an unmarked ventilation shaft.

He had been tracking an eight-point buck. He was setting up to take the shot when he stepped on a wobbly rock and fell backwards into a bush. As he fell, he swung his bow awkwardly, smashing it on a rock. But he was not done falling. Under the bush was a gaping hole, a void, where there should have been solid ground. Somehow Clay had grabbed hold of the side of the hole with his left hand and one of his feet, and hung there like a piece from one of those 'barrel of monkeys' games. Good old 'Spiderman' had nothing on Clay as he clung for his life.

Ed came looking for Clay when he heard Clay calling to him, "Help! I can't hang on much longer!" Ed honed in on the sounds, which had a strangely hollow sound to them. He thought he was getting close when he found some disturbed ground near a strangely out-of-place rhododendron bush, but he saw no trace of the big hunter.

Ed stepped on a wide rock at the base of the bush, and then the rock wobbled. He fell to his knees, almost falling over. Then he saw the hole, and one of Clay's boots hooked awkwardly on the side of the lip.

He grabbed the boot and spread himself out prone, in case the body attached to it suddenly decided to take the plunge into the chasm.

"What kind of shit have you fallen into this time, buddy?" he shouted over the edge.

"Shut the fuck up and get me out of here!" said Clay in desperation.

With his left hand holding Clay's boot to the rock lip, Ed reached his right hand over and grasped Clay's wrist, pulling upward to a point where Clay could get a grip on a rock edge.

Clay was able to clamber up over the side of the edge and sit next to his savior, on the ground under the rhododendron.

"Lost my bow," said Clay.

"You almost lost more than that," chided Ed.

The two men carefully peered over the edge. At first they could only see a few feet into the hole, but as their eyes adjusted to the darkness, they could see deeper into what they saw had been a close call with death for Clay.

"Hey, look! There's your bow, hanging on that ledge," said Ed .

"Yeah. Looks like the stock's splintered real good," Clay said, looking at the shattered bow, the cables and bowstring having recoiled into a bird's nest. "There's no way I'm risking my neck for that crappy piece of shit! This could be the perfect excuse to get an upgrade, maybe one of those Red-Head Blackout bows. They've got them for just five hundred bucks down at the Bass Pro in Concord."

"Fancy schmancy bow. You sure you can handle something like that, with your recently proven prowess?"

"Up yours, Ed!"

"Shit, man, take it easy! You once had a sense of humor. Did you lose that also?" After a moment, Ed questioned, "Okay, what do you figure this hole is?"

"I don't know, but I suspect it's one of those old mines."

"Mining? In this park?"

"No, this would probably be from the eighteen-hundreds, or even older, before they made this a park around 1920 or so."

"I thought this was old Cherokee land?"

"Yeah, but the white man has been taking precious gems and silver out of here since before the seventeen hundreds."

"You think there could be gemstones or silver down there?" asked Ed.

"Sure. You know those tourist places, where you can buy a sack of dirt and pan for rubies and emeralds? Well, where do you think they actually get the stones? They have permits to go up into the back-country, and extract ore."

"Really? I thought mining would be banned in the park."

"Yeah, well, Wildlife Resource Commission guys, those Park Rangers, would shut you down if they found you doing it without a special permit. I think they do it mostly outside of the park, closer to Bryson City, but back in the day they were pulling out rubies and emeralds from this region by the bucket-load. After all, the emerald *is* the official stone of North Carolina," Clay explained. "Heck, some people believe that this region inspired old Frank Baum's idea of the Emerald City in 'The Wizard of Oz', but I think that's just wishful thinking by all the tourist operators up and down the Gorge, especially those clowns at the NOC."

"NOC? What's that?"

"Nantahala Outdoor Center. We passed it on our way up here today. I'll show you on the way out."

"Do you think we should check this out?" asked Ed.

"Can't hurt But not from this shaft. Too dangerous. It could be thirty yards deep for all we know. And there could be all sorts of loose rocks that could fall on us. No, we have to find the main entrance. They're usually filled in with gravel or concrete but some were lost over time and are just hiding behind bushes with no more than an old wooden gate or barricade blocking the entrance," said Clay, playing the local expert.

"Let's get a flash-light and see what we can see from up here, maybe that'll give us an idea as to which direction to look."

When the men returned with a flashlight and peered down from the lip, they saw some wooden beams and garbage strewn around the bottom of the shaft. From what they could see, they were certain that they had discovered an abandoned mine. Visions of riches took hold of them. Whether it was silver, gold, or gemstones, their imaginations conjured up a massive treasure trove.

They eventually found the entrance a few hundred yards downhill from the rhododendron bush. Breaking through a decrepit wooden gate, they discovered that the main entrance was flooded, but the allure of the possible contents of the old mine already possessed them.

The two hunters were quickly transformed into amateur prospectors. They returned to Clay's home in Knoxville, Tennessee, to gather the necessary equipment and supplies to explore the mine. As an avid outdoorsman and occasional placer miner, Clay had much of the needed gear but they still had to rent some of the larger equipment. Ed, an affluent businessman from Atlanta, bankrolled the rest of the operation. Clay and Ed were boyhood friends, and a simple thing like money had never stopped the mutual joy they experienced in each other's company.

Clay knew something about prospecting, having worked in the mining industry. While by no means a geologist, his work in the core shack had taught him a lot about how to examine core and surface chip samples for valuable minerals. He had also spent a lot of time panning gold at his friend's placer claim on Coker Creek, up in Monroe County, Tennessee. He was pretty confident that he could spot valuable gems and some of the more important indicator minerals, and he knew how to use a microscope.

Ed and Clay also knew people they could take samples to for more detailed analysis. So the plan had been to explore the mine, see what they could learn on site, and take samples to a lab in Lawrenceburg, Tennessee, where they could get more detailed analysis done. Of course, all of this had to be done informally, through contacts the two men had, as strictly speaking they would be *poaching*. But that didn't bother Clay and

Ed, who had been deer hunting illegally in the park, and out of season at that, when they found the vent shaft.

All they had to do was to figure out what was valuable in the mine, and start taking the pay-dirt up to Monroe County.

It had been a real adventure at first. Once they had pumped the water out of the first deep dip in the tunnel, which had been completely flooded with crystal clear water, they were able to explore deeper into the tunnel. It sloped downward at first and then leveled off as the tunnel got deeper under the hillside. This meant that the entrance to the mine was a natural water trap. They would have to run the pump on and off throughout the day to keep it from filling back up with water. Some areas farther in, including the intersection of a cross-tunnel with the main tunnel, had been bone dry.

They set up an improvised sample lab in the largest of the intersections, near the rear of the mine where the vent shaft brought fresh air into the mine.

With the generator running most of the time, the tunnels were foul smelling, so taking their coffee and lunch breaks in 'the office' allowed them to take in some fresh clean air. There was even a little bit of natural light coming in, with direct sunlight reaching down into the vent for a few minutes each day.

In the middle of their second day of exploring, Ed was sitting on a pile of old timbers eating lunch as Clay examined a sample under the microscope.

"So Clay, where did you get all these boxes of 'Meals Ready to Eat'?"

"The MREs? I get them from my cousin. He's a reservist with the 591st Transport Company, in Chattanooga."

"So he steals these for you?"

"Not at all. They have to rotate them out when they get near their expiry date on the side of the box."

"But these don't expire for another two months."

"That's not good enough for our troops. They have to have at least six months left or they're considered stale."

"Are they safe to eat?"

"Sure. I keep 'em frozen along with my venison. They'll last for years beyond those dates. But once they thaw out, like these cases over there, they can't be re-frozen again. They'll go punky."

"Well, they're not too bad, anyhow. There is a lot of unnecessary crap in each meal pack that I don't care for, like those rice meals and dried soup packets. And what's with all the powdered sugar drinks?"

"Soldiers like to add those to their canteens, to add sugar to the water when they're humping it on the march. They do generate a lot of garbage, don't they?" Clay said, rhetorically. "But you can't argue with the price!"

The initial excitement and optimism began to wear out after each successive disappointment. At first they had gathered buckets of loose material and taken them out to their campsite, just outside the entrance to the abandoned mine. After panning the loose material, they had been disappointed to find that the mine had not been a gold mine.

After that, they began chipping samples along the tunnel floor, taking them to the lab in the office. Ed would chip off a clean face from the samples and Clay would examine it microscopically

They soon realized that the valuable ore had been removed. So they moved on to taking samples directly from the walls of the tunnel. First they had to drill holes in the rock with the old Pionjar, then hammer in their rock-splitting chisels, and strike the rock hard to cleave off a fresh piece.

What they did not know was that there had been no gold, silver or precious gems to find. The old mine had followed an Olivine seam, which was a mineral that Clay did not have the training to recognize. Even if he had known it, the Olivine would not have proven profitable unless it was going to be mined on a massive scale, as its principal use was as foundry molding sand.

The two men sat on a pile of shoring lumber stacked along the tunnel wall in enjoying one last coffee while they discussed their decision.

"We coming back? - or are we done?" asked Ed.

"Oh, we'll come back for a second round. There definitely is something here, we just don't know what it is! Let's take a few buckets of samples with us and have them assayed by Jacob up in Lawrenceburg. Once we know what sort of mine this was we'll make a new plan and come back," said Clay, confidently.

"So how long will all of that take?"

"At least a month or more before we get assays back. Say another few weeks to get a plan together. We won't be back here for at least a few months, anyhow."

"So it'll fill up again."

"Oh yeah, and that's fine. That'll keep our secret safe."

"We gonna take all the gear out with us today?"

Looking around 'the office', Clay gave it some thought.

"There's no point taking out the MREs, they'll be fine here, and I can't re-freeze them anyhow. We'd better take the lab stuff and all the rented equipment. No point paying for it when we aren't using it. And I have to take the microscope back to the High School or Myrna will get in trouble.

Three hours later, as the men drove off with their equipment and camping gear, there was no sign that they had ever been there. The water level in the tunnel entrance was slowly rising, and the bushes they had roped-off at the entrance to the cave had been released, resuming their former position, once again hiding the entrance to the old mine.

In 4-wheel-drive mode, Clay's pick-up truck bounced and jolted through the ruts and puddles like a bunking bronco, but Clay took care not to make the ride too rough on the equipment tied down in the truck box.

After about two hundred yards, the dirt track joined the much smoother National Forest - Winding Stairs Road, which they followed the half-mile down Queens Creek to Highway 19 and civilization.

As they turned right and headed east along the paved highway past Ferebee Memorial Picnic Area the two men were silent, both feeling very let down.

"Let's pull in to that Relia's Garden place for some lunch," said Ed.

"You're kidding, right?"

"What do you mean, Clay? You don't like Relia's?"

"You want to have a grass-burger or some other kind of organic crap? Not me! I want some red meat and beer. And the last thing I want to do is sit next to some Griswold family of tourists. Let's keep going to Bryson City and go to Bojangles before we head back up through Gatlinburg on the 441."

As if to demonstrate his point, Clay pointed out a red minivan parked at the side of the road, with a family of four standing opposite the Nantahala Outdoor Center's Tourist Information Centre, taking pictures of river-rafting groups floating down the Nantahala River.

"See what I mean? Fuckin' Griswolds!"

"Where?"

"Opposite the NOC," Clay pointed, "Fuckin' Griswolds!"

"HEY! Watch out!" shouted Ed.

A white Econoline van had just pulled out from Silvermine Road, turning left onto Highway 19, cutting directly across their path.

"Asshole!" shouted Clay, braking just enough to avoid T-boning the van.

As Clay and Ed looked at the van, hoping to give the driver an appropriate digital salute, all they got was a momentary glimpse of an orange baseball cap atop the head of a scruffy looking man behind the wheel. Clay thought he saw one of those diamond type beards on the man's chin. He had always hated goatees.

2

THE TALK

Marjorie Carter felt ashamed of herself for what she had just done. She also felt that it would all work out for the best. The problem was that even though she was fairly close with her nine year old daughter she felt very uncomfortable talking about sex with anybody – let alone her own daughter.

Hank was red-faced and angry but held his tongue while Marjorie finished.

"Besides, Hank, you did such a great job having 'The Talk' with Nick back when he turned 13, so I was kind of hoping you would do the same thing with Abby."

"Why does it have to be now? Aren't we busy enough getting ready for the trip?"

"Yeah, I know, but I think we need to talk to her before school tomorrow. There's going to be some kind of Sex Ed class and she's already asking questions. I would rather one of us put the right spin on the whole thing before she and her girlfriends get into it at school tomorrow. And you know how I am about talking with the kids about serious things like that. Will you please take care of it for me?"

With a sigh of resignation Hank accepted the logic.

"OK, but while we talk, I want you to do something for me."

"You name it. What?"

"Those after-dinner dishes I was supposed to clean, and getting the kids to bed tonight."

"Deal!" Marjorie said triumphantly, "And I still got the better part of it!

Twenty minutes later while Hank and Abby were talking in the den, Marjorie was cleaning up the kitchen enthusiastically. She kept looking up the stairs to see if they were done, curious to see the look on her daughter's face after being told about 'the curse'.

Hank tried not to show Abby how pissed off he was about the whole thing, having to deal with a woman's issue. He would have to deal with Marjorie about that later. It was not the first time she had dumped something on him in such a way as to give him no warning – and no choice. So as uncomfortable as he felt about the topic, he pressed ahead with the unpleasant task.

Up in the den, Hank had been asking Abby about school, stalling until he found the right way to broach the topic.

"So what's happening tomorrow?"

"The usual stuff. Phys Ed first, and I have choir practice during lunch-recess. In the afternoon there's some kind of Sex Ed class with a guest teacher from some college."

"And how are things going in the Robotics Team?"

Abby started to pick up on the way Hank was beating around the bush.

"Dad, I'm in the *Junior* Robotics Team. I don't get into the real team until Middle School, next year. But you know this, Daddy. What's really on your mind."

Impressed with her daughter's maturity, Hank pressed on.

"Abby, you'll be turning ten soon, and then next fall you'll be in Middle School. So there are a couple of things we need to talk about."

Abby was quick on the uptake. "You're not giving me 'The Talk', are you, Daddy?" she laughed.

"Well, yes I am," he paused, looking suspiciously at her. "How much of this do you already know?"

"You mean about boys?"

"Actually, that's only part of it. But I wanted to start with the woman part."

"Woman part? Daddy, I'm a *girl*, and I am NOT sexually active. I have no interest in boys, and I think kissing is gross."

"Abby. Do you know what the "Woman's Curse' is?"

"No. Is it doing housework, like Mom does?"

"No. It is something…kind of *bathroom* related."

"What do you mean? Taking showers? Washing hair? That kind of stuff?"

"No, it's more *toilet* related." Hank was getting more and more uncomfortable. He had hoped that Abby had already learned about the menstrual cycle somehow.

"What are you talking about?" Abby frowned, getting frustrated.

"Abby, the 'Woman's Curse' is that every month, I think every four weeks, her body goes through a *change*. Part of that change comes with uncomfortable cramping," he started.

"Cramping? I think I have heard Mom talking about cramps from time to time. Do they hurt?"

"Well, I don't know, but I think they are unpleasant. But that's not all. They also come with other things that are a bit more unpleasant." Hank was about to deliver the worst part.

Abby was a confident and creative child, but had always had a fear of blood and needles. So he wanted to deliver the news in a way that did not terrify her.

"What, Daddy? You're not making any sense."

"Well, when a woman has this monthly change her body has to get rid of some stuff. Kind of like when you have to go to the bathroom, but it's not pee or poop that you have to get rid of."

The look on his face made Abby begin to worry.

"What sort of stuff?"

"Well, blood."

Abby's face went blank, unable to comprehend what her Dad had just said.

"It's not a lot of blood, but there are some things you have to do so that it doesn't make a mess. You can talk to Mom about that part, but I want to explain what it is and why it happens. So when you talk about it at school tomorrow, you will already know it and won't be embarrassed or have to ask questions."

"You mean like when we do that extra math homework, so I am one step ahead of the class? OK, Dad, I understand why you're telling me this," she paused, and then asked "But how does it work?"

Abby was showing both fear and courage simultaneously. It made Hank proud of his little girl. The way she approached life was always like this. No panic, no drama, just a workmanlike rolling up of the sleeves and getting to work on the task. Abby was definitely something of a Tomboy, which caused her some problems with both the boys and the girls at the private school she attended, but it also made Hank and Marjorie confident that their daughter would succeed at anything she put her mind to.

"Yeah, it's like that. So here goes. It is all about babies. You know that women have babies and breast-feed them, and men just go to work and earn money to support them, right?"

Abby nodded.

"And you know men can't have babies, right?"

"Well Duh! You don't have breasts."

"Right. And we don't have *wombs*, either."

"Do I have a womb?" Abby looked intrigued.

"Not exactly. You have not reached puberty yet."

"I know that word. Puberty is when Nick started to grow whiskers and his voice changed, last year, right?"

"Right. Anyhow, girls don't grow whiskers, and their voices don't change."

"But mom plucks hair from her face."

"True, but that's not the point, she won't ever grow a beard, and neither will you. And your voice won't change like Nick's did."

"So what happens when I come down with puberty?"

"Come down with? It's not like getting sick. It's a change you go through, and it takes time, as you grow into more of a woman's body."

Abby stared at her dad, not sure if she was going to like what he was going to say next.

"So the changes you go through, they are all about making it possible for you to have a baby."

"I'm going to have a baby?" she asked, alarmed.

"No! Well, yes, but not for years and years. No, it means your body will begin a long, long, process of one day being *ready* to have a baby. The process starts when you're about ten years old, when you first begin to reach puberty."

"And this change makes blood?" Abby looked afraid now.

"A little bit, once in a while."

"Why?"

"Because the way it works is kind of like," he paused, suddenly at a loss.

"Like what? Dying?"

"No, more like say fruit ripening. You know, like an avocado."

"I get ripe?"

"Something similar to that. As a woman, you have a reproductive system, a baby making system that involves that place in your belly where a baby grows, your womb. But before you are all grown up, it is very small and kind of asleep, like a very small avocado. But when you reach puberty, and 'become a woman', it gets a little bigger. Then each month, it sort of goes ripe. And if you don't start growing a baby in it then at the end of the month your body has to get rid of the contents, like the extra supplies a baby would have needed, and this is what comes out in the bathroom."

"So I get ripe, and then throw it away every month?"

"Kind of like that."

"If that was true, how would my body know what day it is?" asked Abby, triumphantly.

"Well, your body gets in tune with the moon or something, and goes through this cycle when it is right for you, but usually around every 28 days."

"So it's not by calendar?"

"No, the moon has a two-week cycle, so 28 days from full moon to full moon."

"Like a Werewolf?" Abby was looking a bit more relaxed, but still very keen to understand the whole thing.

"No," said Hank, barely suppressing a smile. "A werewolf goes through its changes on a full moon. Women don't. At least, I don't think so. You'll have to ask your mom about that."

"OK. So how do I do it? How do I get rid of my avocado?"

"You will feel some kind of cramps and a bloated feeling."

"What does bloated mean?"

"It means kind of filled up with water. Your face, your legs, all of your body will hold on to some extra water, just before you have your period."

"My period?"

"Yeah, that's what it's called. Like a werewolf has a curse put on it, sometimes women think of this as a sort of woman's curse."

"Why is it called a period?"

"I don't know. Maybe because it lasts for a period of time."

"How long?"

"I think five days, or a week."

"You mean I am going to bleed for a week?" Abby was suddenly very distressed, "From where? – my bum?"

"Sort of. You will have a small amount of blood, not from your bum, but in front, where you pee, for about a week. And you'll have those cramps and that bloated feeling. You will also be very cranky."

"Cranky?" Abby thought about it for a second. "Yes, Dad, I will be *very* cranky if that ever happens to me. Can't I make it not happen? Can I go to a doctor and make it not happen to me?"

"Sorry, sweetie, you can't. But it's not all bad."

"What's good about it?" Abby asked, doubtfully.

"Well, ask Mom some time why being a woman is better than being a man. She'll probably tell you that having a baby – what a man can't do – is very special. The most important thing you could possibly experience in life."

"I know about that. And I want to have babies one day, but not for a long time."

"That's the other part of it, Abby."

"There's more? Daddy, I don't like this." Tears started coming to her eyes as she feared that her father was going to give her even worse news, but Hank had to continue.

"Along with having your period, when a girl enters puberty, she has other changes.

"Like what? I'm already going to be a cranky werewolf. What else is going to happen to me?"

"Well, two things, I think. First, your body will start to change shape. Your hips will get bigger, and you will start to grow breasts."

"You mean like some of the fat girls in school?"

"Not exactly fat. Well, maybe a little. But it's more about getting a curvy, woman's body instead of the skinny, straight body you have now. It does not mean you have to get fat. But I guess some of the girls you know, who eat at McDonalds a lot, have had bodies with more curves and maybe even breasts for years now. But that does not mean that they have reached puberty."

"So when do I reach puberty? When I get fat and have big hips and breasts, or when I start to bleed? And what's the other thing that's going to happen?" Abby seemed to be getting angry at her father for telling her all of this, as though it was his fault.

"The other thing is that you may start to become interested in boys."

"They are *not* interesting. Well, maybe some of them are fun, but they just talk about war and football. What could be interesting about that?"

"No, I mean interested in having them look at you. Like you may want them to notice you. Or more like maybe kiss you."

"I don't want them to kiss me! Yuk!"

"I'm happy you feel that way. But here's the thing. Some of the seniors in school, like some of the football players, chase some of the younger girls. And these boys have reached puberty – in a big way."

"What do you mean?"

"I mean, they want to have sex with girls."

"You mean, like 'blowjob' and 'orgasm'?"

"Abby, where did you hear those words? And don't say them out loud. It's enough that you know them, but do you know what they mean?" asked Hank, trying not to react to the jolt he just received from his only little girl.

"Not really, something about sex and penises. Everybody says those things but I don't think even they know *exactly* what they mean. What *do* they mean?"

Well, in general, they are words about having sex. Do you know what that is?" Hank felt very awkward about what he was going to have to explain, but then Abby made it easier for him.

"Well, I think it's what you and Mom do when you are 'fooling around' with each other."

"That's right. I don't want to get into the details, but the important thing is that you are not allowed to do that, not until you are over 18. Ideally, not until you are married, but a lot of kids in school start doing it way too soon."

"Yeah, I've heard about some of them who are doing it. They brag about it, and lots of them are lying, like Nick lies about it."

"You would be surprised. Did you know that some of the girls at the Academy have gotten pregnant?"

"Yeah. And I think that's what Mrs. Ferguson wants that guest teacher to talk to us about, tomorrow." Abby seemed to have gotten over the hard part of the discussion, which made Hank feel a lot better.

"I'm sure that she'll tell you a lot more about it than I can. But the point is you are going to go through puberty and start to become a woman. When this starts to happen, I want you to be open and honest with me and with your Mom. You will start making special friends with some boys, maybe even start dating them, eventually, but absolutely you must not have sex."

"OK, Dad, I won't have sex."

"I mean it. Not because it would upset me or your mother but because it would take away from your future. Having sex leads to having babies and you need to do a few other things first with your life. You need to go to university, travel the world, have some adventures, and when the time is right, then think of marriage and planning have a family."

"But you and Mom have sex, and Mom doesn't have any more babies."

"Yes, that's true. And maybe Mrs. Ferguson will talk to you about that as well. That's called 'birth control'. And when you actually do become sexually active you have to know all about birth control and how to protect yourself from sexually transmitted diseases."

"You mean like getting the flu from each other?"

"No! Sexually transmitted diseases can give you problems for the rest of your life. They can even make it impossible to have children. And some, like HIV Aids, can eventually kill you."

"Then I am definitely not going to have sex."

"That's a good approach, Abby", Hank almost choked as he realized that he was explaining abstinence to his nine year old daughter. "But the real thing I wanted you to know about all of this is that you can talk to me, and talk to your mother about this stuff. We won't get angry about it. You can trust us. We are all in this together, as a family, and we support whatever decisions you make with your life."

"Ok, Dad. I understand," Abby said, with a growing hint of sadness in her voice and on her face as she worked through the implications of what it really meant to be cursed.

"Now I think you should go and talk to Mom about what to do when you have your first period, when you bleed for the first time. I don't want to talk about those girlie details, ever!"

Abby got up quietly and climbed into her father's lap, almost as if she wanted to go back to a time when she was a little girl and did not have to deal with such terrible things as puberty and bleeding.

Hank embraced her, holding her gently, somehow understanding how difficult the conversation must have been for her.

With her head nestled into her father's shoulder, curled up like a cat, Abby showed Hank just how smart and resilient she was.

"Daddy, I understand that this stuff we talked about was not easy for you either. I just want to be a little girl a while longer, and not grow up so fast, OK?"

"OK, cupcake."

"Will you sing to me?" she said, choking back some tears, in grief over what she felt was the end of her childhood.

With a gruff voice at first, and then increasingly musical and soothing, Hank began to sing one of the songs he used to sing to her as a toddler. It was a song he had invented for Abby when she was just a baby, to the rhythm of The Happy Wanderer:

"I love my little Abigail, my darling little girl, and as I go, I love to sing, my Abby on my back. Abbigee, Abbigaa, Abbigee, Abbeygaa -ha -ha -ha -ha -ha -ha -aaabbigee, Abbigaa. My Abby on my back."

After a few more minutes cuddling with her dad, Abby's curiosity took hold and she got up to go and interrogate her mother over the practical mechanics of the Woman's Curse.

Hank sat there for a moment, wishing he could go back to when Abby was smaller and sing another of their songs to her, but the special moment was over. His duty completed successfully, Captain Hank Carter got up from his armchair and went over to the liquor cabinet and poured himself a stiff drink. As a C-130 Hercules pilot with the 94th Airlift Wing, at Dobbins Air Force Base in Atlanta, Hank had been put to the test as a military officer on more significant missions than he could count, but taking on 'The Talk' had been one of the more terrifying experiences of his life.

As the single-malt whiskey burned its way down his throat with a satisfying effect on his mind, he reflected on how the conversation had gone.

His pride in his daughter grew even stronger that night. Not so much because she knew anything about the topic, but by the way she had taken the terrible truth in stride and did not panic about the blood. Hank Carter mused to himself - Abby always had such an aversion to blood. It barely seemed to affect her tonight. My baby girl is going away and I can do nothing to hold on to this innocent child.

With such thoughts roiling in his head, Captain Henry Carter of the USAF treated himself to a return engagement to his liquor cabinet.

"My daughter is truly a remarkable girl," Hank said out loud as he carried his double Canadian Club to his favorite chair, closed his eyes, and shut out the world.

3

ROAD TRIP

Hank was not sure but it seemed to him that Abby was already carrying herself with more maturity. As though she was no longer a child, and yet she was still just nine years old. According to Marjorie there was absolutely no sign of Abby having reached puberty. The pamphlet that Abby had brought home from the Sex Ed lecture at Pace Academy stated that the onset of puberty in girls was generally around nine or ten years old, so Marjorie's decision to broach the topic had been timely.

As it was, she and Abby had really gotten closer somehow by having had a woman to woman talk about such things. That Hank had done the heavy lifting had made the whole enterprise get off to a good start. To Marjorie, the chaos of packing up the family and heading out for their spring break road trip had seemed easy in comparison, and she was grateful to Hank for doing his part.

"Hank? Have you finished loading the roof-topper?"

"Just about. Just have to put the sleeping bags in. Do you know where they are?"

"Yeah. I had Nicky put them in the bin in the trailer. You want me to get them?"

"You got them to fit? I thought it was already full in there."

"Nope. We made space by moving the firewood into the stow-and-go spaces under the seats in the minivan. All we have left to pack is the extra water carrier and the food, and I got all the food to fit into just *two* Roughnecks. They're ready. Can you take them out for me now?"

Hank shut the car-topper and then got down from the ladder. He looked back at his handiwork. To anybody else it might look a bit haphazard, with four bicycles strapped to the roof-rack just behind the car-topper atop the family's Dodge Caravan, and the rough looking old pop-up tent-trailer hooked up to the bumper, but to Hank it looked all squared away.

After packing away the Roughneck bins and a few last-minute items into the rear of the minivan, they were ready to go.

"Shotgun! Called Nick, racing past Abby and Marjorie to take the passenger seat. He was already strapped in and unfolding the map by the time the girls got into their seats. The back row of seats was folded down to make more space for their suitcases, camping gear and food. Hank settled into the driver's seat and adjusted the rear-view mirror. There was a small but sufficient gap through the gear, allowing him an acceptable tunnel to the rear window.

"OK, copilot, give me directions for the first leg of the journey. But be advised, we rotate in the cruise pilot into your seat as soon as we enter North Carolina, got it?"

"Affirmative, Captain!" said Nick. "But dad, will you let me do some driving when we get to our campsite? – On some of those back-country dirt roads?"

"We'll see. You remember what happened last time!"

"But that wasn't my fault! The ruts were soft, that's why we got stuck."

"No, the ruts were typical, and the problem was that you didn't *listen*. When I said 'keep going, don't stop', you shouldn't have stopped right then in the middle of the puddle. We would have had enough momentum to get through it, but stopping..."

"Listen to you guys, we haven't even gotten out of the driveway and you're being the Bickersons again!"

"OK. We'll call it a draw. But next time I let you drive, you had better be a voice-activated automaton and do exactly what I say, got it?"

"Yes, Dad."

"Just like when Coach Robison calls in a play during practice, you follow the playbook, right?"

"OK, OK, I got it. Can we go now?"

"I'm still waiting for directions, Copilot."

"OK, let's get the show on the road. First, drive out the driveway, turn right onto Highland, and follow it to Spring Road. Take a left on Spring Road, and go right onto Village Parkway. Just like going to the base, Dad. OK so far?"

"Yup. Good start. Now set it up on the GPS."

While Nick punched buttons onto the GPS, Hank drove the same route he drove to his unit at Dobbins AFB. Being on autopilot allowed him to think a few moves ahead of his copilot.

"OK, now turn right on Windy Hill, and cross I-75, and then get onto I75 Northbound."

"Well said, Nick. But there's a problem with your route."

"Why?"

"We're not going through Blue Ridge," said Hank, wryly, as he passed the I-75 Northbound on-ramp and just kept going along Windy Hill, into Sandy Springs.

"So what's our route?"

"We have to stop in Franklin, to drop off a package for a friend from the base," said Hank.

"Franklin? Where's that?" asked Nick, fumbling with the paper map.

"That's your problem. Try to get on-mission, son, we've got a payload to deliver!" Hank said, trying to provoke Nick.

Fifteen minutes later they were on their way up Highway 23 approaching Gainesville when Nick finally caught up.

"OK, Dad. It's all programmed. It will add thirty miles and forty-five minutes to the trip."

"And how much fuel, in pounds?"

"Aw, I don't know how to calculate that, Dad. But I think about a gallon or two."

"Well done, closer to two gallons. Great job, Nick. You'd be surprised at how many of the pipeline pilots coming off the Jayhawk at JSUPT couldn't do what you've just done!"

"Thanks Dad. Whatever 'JSUPT' means."

"That's the Joint Specialized Undergraduate Pilot Training school. New pilots come to the Wing after flying the Jayhawk jet in Columbus. Come on, Nick, I thought you knew all this."

"Sure, Dad, but I get mixed up with all your Air Force jargon, you know." It meant a lot to Nick whenever he could get praise of any kind from his Dad. It seemed to Nick that the lion's share of attention always went to Abby, except for the football. Nick knew how hard it was for his Dad to juggle his missions and other assignments so that he could be there for the home games of the Pace Knights, Nick's football team. That was one area where he had his Dad all to himself. Abby was too busy with her own life to ever come along to one of his football games.

After dropping off the package for Hank's retired Air Force buddy in Franklin, North Carolina, Nick rotated to the back seat so that Marjorie could ride in front.

They stopped a few times along the way, making a good six hour drive out of the one hundred and sixty mile route. But that was fine for Hank and Marjorie. Getting there was half the fun. Besides, they didn't have to meet their guide, Rob, at the Nantahala Outdoor Center, until three o'clock. They had plenty of time to kill.

With the kids intently listening to music on their iPods, Marjorie and Hank were able to talk without worrying about the kids picking up too much of their conversation.

"Are you sure we're ready for Level III rapids, Hank?"

"Sure. Those level II rapids in Pisgah last summer were a blast, and the kids had no problem with them. Besides, they'll be wearing life jackets and helmets, and there are lots of other rafts on the river all the time. We'll be fine."

"It looked pretty dramatic on those You-tube videos."

"The kids are both strong swimmers, and I'm sure Rob will give us a thorough safety briefing about the route. And it's actually a long way from our take-out point to those big rocks and the falls. And the last stretch is wide and slow. Major Duhig told me all about it, He did it with his kids last fall. We'll have no problem getting out. We'll stop there and take some pictures when we meet with Rob tonight. You'll see," said Hank.

"I guess. And Abby really is a strong swimmer now. And I don't have any worries about Nick, he's grown so much!"

"Yeah, he's almost as tall as I am. He's going to be six-four at least, perfect size for a cornerback or a safety"

"You men and your football. I wish you would get Nick interested in something less dangerous, like golf or basketball."

"Oh don't worry, he'll outgrow football soon enough. He's doing well in his math and sciences, and he has a good head on his shoulders. But I want him in football a bit longer, while he works through his growing spurts and puberty. Keep him busy and he'll stay out of trouble. He doesn't have much time left, you know. He'll be in Grade 10 soon, can you believe it? And Abby's not far behind."

"I know. It's happened so fast. I want them to stay young just a little while longer. But I'm afraid that this may be the last time that they'll really enjoy just hanging around with us, camping and sitting around by the fire."

"Yeah," Hank looked meaningfully at Marjorie. "Our babies are growing up so fast. Soon enough they'll be out there on their own, without us around to take care of them all the time."

"They still need us, Hank. At least we've got that!"

4

EXPERT WITNESS

The strain on the woman's face made her look older than her forty-two years. That she was having problems finding the Macon County courthouse, in Franklin, North Carolina, was not the cause of her strain. It went far deeper than that.

Even the thought of being late for the trial did not disturb her all that much. All that Mary Freeman really wanted was the chance to look at the man who had murdered her husband and taken a loving father away from a young boy.

"Mom, I think I see it!" said her 11-year old son. "Those flagpoles! There's a little sign there saying 'Courthouse'," he said, of the unusual brick building. They had driven right past it a few times, getting the addresses mixed up, going on to 5 East Main Street rather than stopping at what looked more like a fire hall or perhaps a theatre than a courthouse, but was in fact, 5 West Main Street.

On her previous appearances, she had been taken to the courthouse by old Jack Freeman, but the trial had worn the old man down. He was simply too weak to accompany her, to give her strength. Without her father-in-law, she had to find the courthouse for herself. It drove home the fact that now she truly was on her own. Feeling completely alone now, she found the small town to be an alien place. Without her husband of sixteen years, her compass, and now the loss of his father as her guide, she was driving in a mental fog.

"Oh, yeah, I see. Good Job, Jared," she said.

After parking and walking past the flags, she paused with her son in the shade of the young trees in front of the entrance, gathering her thoughts.

She felt her heart begin to race as the reality dawned on her. She would sit with her son to watch a full day of testimony. It was day 18 in the murder trial, and she had attended a few times earlier in the trial, but those had seemed to be all about pointless legal maneuvering and complicated discussions that she did not understand. But today was different, the testimony of the psychiatrist and that of the arresting officer was going to take place.

From what she had read in the paper these were the most important elements in the case, so she wanted to be here to watch the reaction on the face of her husband's murderer as the final two witnesses were called to the stand to seal his fate.

Soon enough, she reasoned, the North Carolina Superior Court judge would come down with the guilty verdict. It would be enough that Jared would have seen the monster at least once, and have a chance to listen to some of the damning evidence. She did not plan to bring Jared back for the final judgment or the sentencing. She planned to save that for herself. But she felt that it would be critical to Jared's healing process to see at least some of the trial in person, so that he could begin to understand that there was a measure of retributive justice in the system. She had no doubt that the judge would find the evil man guilty, the evidence was so overwhelming.

As it was, she had made it into the courtroom in time and then found seats close enough to the front, where she could get a good look across at the defendant. It did not take long for the proceedings to get underway.

"All rise! Macon County Superior Court is now in session. Judge Lewis Durbin presiding. Case Number 12 dash 749 continued from yesterday, State of North Carolina versus David M. Seiprecht," said the court clerk loudly.

"Be seated," said Judge Durbin as he settled into the large leather chair behind his bench.

"Are you ready to call your next witness, counselor?"

"We are, your honor. Prosecution calls Dr. Kevin Peel."

All eyes turned towards the back of the room to watch as the large doors were opened by an attendant from the Macon County Sheriff's Department. The deputy looked a bit nervous as he pulled the door open and held it for the well-dressed little man who entered a few seconds later.

Macon County Sheriff Albie Singer was seated in the back row, as much to monitor the public audience as to observe the behavior of the troubled young deputy assigned to 'door duty'.

Deputy Martin had been on Sergeant Clifton's D-shift but had received too many complaints from his fellow officers. It was not that he was argumentative or noncooperative, but rather that he simply did not fit in and they wanted him out of their unit.

Sheriff Singer thought that it had more to do with the man's somewhat effeminate nature than anything else. Officially, the sexual orientation of his personnel was not a concern, but Sheriff Singer thought that Deputy Martin might be more comfortable amongst the C-Shift where he could be relegated to the Honor - Guard detail, and avoid the grist mill of the more operational assignments.

Thinking about Deputy Martin, Sheriff Singer hardly glanced at the man in the tweed jacket who strode confidently to the witness box to take his pledge to tell the truth.

After Dr. Kevin Peel was sworn in, he polished his eyeglasses as his qualifications as an expert witness were being established. Then the prosecutor began his line of questioning in earnest.

"Can you tell us, Dr. Peel, have you had a chance to interview the defendant?"

"Yes, I have, on several occasions."

"And have you formed a diagnosis?"

"Yes, of course. That's why I was called in by your office."

"And I have read your diagnosis.. But for those of us who don't understand the language you use as a psychiatrist, could you explain it in layman's terms?"

"By all means. I'll do my best. Mr. Seiprecht is ill. He suffers from an erotic obsession focused on young children. That is well documented, and in my observations, his designation as a registered sexual offender is entirely warranted."

"I see. And in your expert opinion, is he a psychopath?"

"Well, actually, my diagnosis was that he is a sociopath."

"Sorry, Dr Peel. The court has already heard the testimony of Dr. Bell, the attending psychiatrist at the remand facility, who described Mr. Seiprecht as a psychopath. So for the benefit of those of us who are not experts, could you explain the distinction?"

"With pleasure," said Dr. Peel, drawing more than a few raised eyebrows. "Dr. Bell's diagnosis was thoroughly supported by his findings. However there is dispute within the medical community as to the role a subject's conscience plays in the subject's personality and how it manifests in their antisocial behavior. While Dr. Bell's work is sound, he is old school. We no longer actually use the term 'psychopath' in today's psychiatric diagnostic manuals, while of course the term is still commonly used by mental health professionals and laypersons. Technically, we now use a variety of more accurate terms."

The eyes of the prosecutor, judge and most of the audience began to glaze over as the somewhat excited Dr. Peel went on.

"I take the view, consistent with the Hare Psychopathy Checklist, that both sociopaths and psychopaths have absolutely no regard for the rights or feelings of others, and this feature is consistently present in criminal behavior. First indications begin to appear in adolescence, such as self-serving behavior, disregard for rules, escalating risk-seeking behavior and so on. Eventually they progress to bullying behavior, cruelty to animals, and disregard for the law. Both psychopaths and sociopaths lack empathy and conscience, and do not experience feelings like guilt or remorse. It is not that they do not care about other's feelings, they simply do not have the ability to feel anything themselves, so they are incapable of imagining how they may make others feel."

"So what is the difference?" asked the prosecutor, impatient with Dr. Peel's long explanation.

"I am coming to that. It is all about the degree to which a subject's personality is *organized*. The sociopath is less organized, more spontaneous, and more likely to be a social outcast."

"Why is that, Dr.?"

"Because they do not have the intelligence and self-control of a true psychopath. You see, a psychopath tends to be much more organized, and has developed the ability to mask his antisocial nature by mimicking the behavior of what you might call 'normal' people. So a psychopath could fit in well in any community, with nobody suspecting their true nature. They tend to be successful and well educated, typically drawn to high paying professions. This is in sharp contrast to the sociopath, who tends to fail at just about everything. A great many of them wind up turning to military service, short term employment, or social dependency. Anecdotally, as I have not yet published my own findings, I can also tell you that only the top 20% turn out to be psychopaths, and the lower 80% is where the sociopaths predominate, as determined by the *Hare Psychopathy Checklist* and my own, perhaps more precise, *Peel Personality Inventory* test."

"Why do you describe the psychopaths as the 'top'?"

"Simply because they are more....developed. You see, even if their urges have a similar basis – whether socially derived or whether it is a specific neurological disorder present from birth – psychopaths are considered to be far more capable than the sociopaths. They are intelligent and crafty, and often devise sophisticated, well-planned schemes to satisfy their need to hurt others, take from others, or in some other way serve themselves. That is why they make for successful criminals."

"So they wind up in prison, by and large?"

"No, not at all. They are the ones who do not get caught. Whether a youthful prank of breaking a window at school, a serious, violent crime, or even white collar crime on Wall Street, the psychopath will have devoted his or her considerable intellectual capabilities to making sure someone else takes the blame, and that his own tracks are well covered."

"And in the case of a sociopath, then, he will not have done such planning in advance?"

Smiling as though a student were finally showing a glimmer of understanding, Dr. Peel excitedly replied: "Correct! That is why I support the general view that the vast majority of inmates suffering from APD -"

"I'm sorry, Doctor," interrupted the prosecutor, "APD?"

"Antisocial Personality Disorder, which is a medical illness that needs to be treated, much like Post-Traumatic-Stress-Disorder, which has finally become recognized as a medical problem that requires treatment and a degree of compassionate understanding."

"Go on, about the criminal behavior of these APD sufferers."

"So in the case of the sociopathic personality, they are more likely to have made a spontaneous outburst that lead to a criminal act, not have thought it through or figured out how to cover their tracks, and wind up being arrested. So they tend to have long criminal records, of essentially stupid acts that one should have been able to get away with, with just a modicum of thought applied."

"I see. So you are saying that Mr. Seiprecht, as a sociopath, is prone to unplanned, sudden outbursts? With no concern for the effect on others?"

"Quite. And my view is substantiated by Mr. Seiprecht's long criminal record, as I am sure you now understand," Dr. Peel said, condescendingly.

Even though Dr. Peel's testimony was central to the conclusion of the prosecutor's case, and he was happy with the results that line of questioning had drawn out, he was starting to find Dr. Peel to be a very unpleasant and egotistical man.

He moved on to the next line of questioning.

"But what about his temperament? Is he an angry person?"

"Not at all. He is a coward. That is why he is attracted to children. They are unlikely to present a threat to him and he can therefore exercise unlimited power over them."

This seemed to throw the prosecutor off for a moment.

"But you have just testified, in general mostly, as to the antisocial behavior and the spontaneous nature of the sociopath.

If we can focus specifically on the defendant, do you mean to say that Mr. Seiprecht is *incapable* of violence towards an adult?"

"Yes. He would do anything he could to avoid confrontation with an adult, especially a large man, like the victim in this case."

"Objection, your honor!" exclaimed the prosecutor, looking confused and upset.

"Mr. Yost, you can't object to your own witness! He is *your* expert witness, remember," said the judge, amused. To many in the gallery, it was clear that Judge Durbin and Mr. Yost had some bad blood from previous encounters in the courtroom. The Judge seemed to enjoy watching Yost suffer at the hands, or words, of his own witness.

"Your honor, I request that his remarks be stricken from the record"

"On what grounds?"

"On the grounds that this testimony contradicts what was in the written report, and the testimony last week, by the prison residential psychiatrist, Dr. Bell, and also contradicts Dr. Peel's own report, which is also on record.

"What are you saying, counselor? Come out with it!"

"I am saying that Dr. Peel has... That he is a *hostile witness*," he said, with increasing anger.

"He's *your* witness, you'll have to run with it. I will determine whether Dr. Peel is a hostile witness or is not, based upon his further testimony. You do have more questions, do you not?" asked the judge, adding his own fuel to the fire.

The prosecutor tried to salvage his case, soldiering on.

"Dr. Peel. Isn't it true that when you filed your preliminary report you stated that Mr. Seiprecht had exhibited all the classical signs of an antisocial personality? And that he had, and I quote, 'generalized anger and antisocial frame of reference,' – end-quote?"

"Yes, that's correct. Those were my findings, and that is consistent with what I have been explaining to you."

The prosecutor ignored that jab and continued. "And your initial interview was conducted within what, forty-eight hours of Mr. Seiprecht's arrest?"

"Yes."

"So, shortly after he was arrested with the murder weapon in his possession, with the deceased's blood on his clothing and in his vehicle, presumably after dumping a corpse…"

"Objection!" said the defense lawyer, looking at the judge with a look that said: 'do I even need to say it?'

"Sustained!"

"I'll re-phrase. Shortly after having been arrested and charged with Murder, Mr. Seiprecht had appeared to you to be something of a dangerous, ill-tempered person, correct?"

"Well, those are your words, not mine, but yes, that captures the spirit of my *initial* assessment."

"And in subsequent interviews and assessments of Mr. Seiprecht, was this not confirmed?"

"Quite the opposite in fact."

"How so?"

"I was wrong."

"Could you please explain?"

"That assessment was made based on not knowing the patient's history. But after the initial screening, I dug into the extensive medical file on David and came to understand his problems in a more complete manner. So I updated my diagnosis. It's all there in the appendix to the final report."

The prosecutor had missed that. He had only skimmed the final report, confirming that the required number of sessions with the court-appointed psychiatrist had been conducted, that all the 'I's were dotted and 'T's crossed. He had assumed that the psychiatrist's report would help build the case that David Seiprecht was an angry, violent man. A psychopath who had committed murder in the first degree. A strong feeling of discomfort was building in Yost's brain, accompanied by an acid taste in the back of his throat.

"So you are now saying, what? That he is not prone to violence?"

"He is capable of violence, to be sure. And he is an angry man, certainly, but due to the abuse he suffered as a child, the neglect he experienced in his formative years, and due to the post-traumatic stress disorder he developed during his military service in the Second Gulf

War, he had become a fearful, timid man who can only feel power if he is in control of a child or perhaps an invalid or an elderly person. He is prone to antisocial outbursts, certainly, and has therefore come to live on the fringes of society, in a sense hiding from the world. He is a sociopath, remember. But he is not capable of fighting with, let alone killing a grown man of the size and stature of the victim. He simply could not do such a thing. The most likely thing he would have been capable of would be some sort of verbal insult, then he probably would have run away. There simply would be no advantage for him in a confrontation with a man as tough and confident as we have heard that Mr. Freeman was."

"Your honor, I once again ask that the court declare Dr. Peel a hostile witness. His revisions to the psychiatric report and recantation of his earlier testimony during discovery are clearly in opposition to his role as an expert witness for the prosecution. No further questions for you, Mr. Peel," said the prosecutor, dismissively.

"That's *Dr. Peel*, if you don't mind," said the psychiatrist, with a slight upward curling of the corners of his mouth.

Prosecutor Yost thought to himself – *God, please! Don't let me puke!*

The disastrous testimony of the psychiatrist had been a major blow to the prosecutor's case, but at least he had the arresting officer to aid him in wrapping things up. Shortly into his testimony, the Macon County Sheriff's Senior Investigative Detective dropped a bombshell.

"Detective Sergeant Fraser, can you confirm that the blood found in the trunk of Mr. Seiprecht's vehicle was that of the victim?"

"Yes. Or we *thought* so. But then we found... administrative errors."

"Administrative errors?" asked the prosecutor, incredulously.

"Yes. There was a break in the chain."

"The chain?"

"Yes, the chain of evidence. It started with the deputy who had been first at the scene. He had been tasked with sitting on the car – that is to say *to stay with the car* – until it was processed by the team from the crime lab."

"And how long was that?"

"Not long, perhaps an hour. But Deputy Martin and his more junior partner did not stay put. They left their post so that Deputy Martin could use the washroom at a gas station, about a half-mile from where the arrest had been made."

Astonished with the new information, the prosecutor made the fatal mistake of asking a question for which he did not know the answer. "How long was the vehicle left unattended?"

"About fifteen minutes. Isn't that right, Deputy?" asked Detective Sergeant Fraser, casting his deep voice across the courtroom. At the back of the courtroom young Deputy Martin cringed as much from the shame of his own negligence as from the glare from Sheriff Singer seated just a few feet from him in the back of the room.

This all came as a complete shock for the Prosecutor. In the few seconds of red-faced silence that hung in the air of the courtroom like a potent mixture of gasoline and oxygen, anybody could see that Yost was about to explode.

The problem was he did no know who to blame. *Had he done a pis-poor job of deposing the witness on the initial interview and during Discovery? – Or had the Detective Sergeant been holding out on him? How could such a major break in the chain of custody only appear now, in the final stages of the trial?* Yost thought to himself, uncertain of whom to lay the blame upon or what to do next.

It didn't matter which, as Yost knew in his heart that it was his own fault for failing to remember the cardinal rule about witnesses, clients, and people in general. They are always holding out on you and they are always lying about something.

With his entire case blown apart due to the negligence of the police and the 180 degree turn in the psychiatrist's testimony, the prosecutor had then stumbled awkwardly through his final summary.

Without the hammer and nails that the last two witnesses had been expected to provide, the summary of the physical evidence had been next to useless given the break in the chain of custody of what should have been damning evidence.

That the accused was a registered sexual offender with a long history of charges of sexual assault, stalking, breaking and entering, and at least one conviction for unlawful confinement had somehow been converted into a *defense* in that his traits were those of a cowardly little creature who could therefore not have beaten the much larger victim to death.

For the defense, it had been a watershed moment. They had been on the verge of proposing a plea-bargain the night before, when going over their case with the accused. For his part, the accused Mr. Seiprecht had been surprisingly confident that he did not need to make a deal. It seemed as though he had an inkling that the prosecutor's case would disintegrate at the last minute.

While the defense lawyers congratulated themselves and the shackles were removed from the defendant's wrists, the distraught wife of the murder victim did not comprehend what had just happened.

"What do you mean, not guilty?" she asked a man sitting in the row in front of her.

"Judge Durbin threw the case out. Without the physical evidence, and with what the psychiatrist said, the prosecutor has no case. So the man walks, regardless of how guilty he looked."

She was in shock. Her son, understanding that the man who had brutally beaten his father to death for no apparent reason, was bewildered. He stared at the now free man who walked past him towards the exit at the back of the courtroom. Seiprecht gave Jared a smug, cruel smile that somehow conveyed an evil promise, all in a single glance.

Herman Yost finally made it to a toilet stall, but vomited all over his expensive shoes. *There goes the partnership*, he thought, as he dabbed the mess off of his shoes with toilet paper.

Five minutes later the taxi taking David Seiprecht out of town turned north on Harrison Avenue and headed northbound into the countryside on Bryson County Road.

Ever vigilant for police cruisers, David Seiprecht watched as Sergeant Fraser passed the taxi and sped away to the north. Seiprecht wasn't afraid of Sergeant Fraser, or any cop for that matter.

"Let me off at the next intersection," David said to the cabby, and then the taxi slowly pulled to the edge of the road. As he watched the taxi make a U-turn and head back to Franklin, David relished the taste of freedom and the excitement he felt.

He didn't turn around at the sound of the car that pulled up next to him, nor was he surprised to hear someone addressing him. It was all going according to plan.

"That was close! You're really going to have to make it up this time," said the voice.

"Don't worry. I've got something special in mind. You'll love it," David Seiprecht said, turning towards the driver.

5

NANTAHALA GORGE

When they reached the Great Smoky Mountains Expressway, about four miles west of Bryson City, North Carolina, Hank decided to pull into the service station to top up the gas tank.

He pulled into an inner lane and drove forward to the front pump, leaving room for a vehicle immediately behind him. He looked in his rear-view mirror and saw that the white Econoline van that entered the service station right after him had pulled off to the right, near the propane filling area.

"Everybody out! Pee break! You guys go ahead and use the washroom and then we'll meet in the shop and get an ice cream," said Hank.

"Thanks, Dad!" said the kids, with enthusiasm.

Hank filled the tank while Marjorie poked around in the small food store portion of the service station and the kids used the bathrooms outside. As he was filling the tank, Hank looked across the parking lot at a motor-home with Georgia plates pulling up to the pumps in the outside lane, to his left. A family much like his own began spilling out. There were two younger boys and a slightly older daughter, perhaps the same age as Abby, maybe a little older.

As he watched the other family head into the food store, he wondered how much a motor-home like that would cost and what it would be like to just drive up to the campsite and park, unhook a small car from the bumper, and be ready to go just like that. He had to admit it had a certain appeal. Then he told himself that he preferred 'real' camping, setting up the pop-up tent and making up the beds and getting out all the camping paraphernalia. Then he told himself that perhaps in his retirement years, when the kids were gone, when his back gave out and his breath grew short, that wimpy lifestyle might appeal to him.....suddenly he was day-dreaming.

When Abby entered the grimy bathroom, on the far side of the gas station, near the propane tanks, her eyes adjusted to the darkness. After doing her business, she got up and washed her hands in the sink. The towel dispenser was empty but there was another machine beside it.

The door suddenly opened. At first Abby could not make out the silhouette coming at her, the bright sunlight blinding her. She then realized that it was just another young girl, like herself, coming in to use the bathroom.

After the door closed behind the girl, Abby turned her attention back to the machine. The girl walked right up beside her, put a quarter into the machine and turned the knob. Suddenly a small white package popped out.

"Need a tampon?" the girl asked Abby. She seemed to be about the same age. The bright yellow halter top she was wearing seemed to make the most out of her breasts, as though she was proud of her sprouts and wanted to show the little buds off.

"Uh, no thanks. I was just trying to figure out what kind they were." Abby bluffed her way through the explanation. She knew what tampons were, because her mother had shown her one a couple of days ago, but had never noticed a tampon dispensing machine before.

"Suit yourself. I've just started getting my period, but I'm getting used to it. Have you had yours yet?" the girl asked, nonchalantly.

"Nope. What grade are you in?"

"I'm in grade six, at Riverside in East Point, in 'Lanta. How 'bout you?"

"I'm in grade five, at Pace Academy."

"Ooh La La. You must be rich."

"Nope. My Dad says he can't really afford it, but Grandpa is helping pay for it. My name is Abby Carter, what's your name?" Abby said to the unusual looking girl.

"Emily. Emily Harper. Nice to meet you, Abby. So what are you doing in the 'Nanny'? Are you going water rafting, or on your way back to 'Lanta?"

"We're just arriving. We're camping tonight, then going rafting tomorrow. How 'bout you?"

"We're on our way home," she said, and then entered the bathroom stall.

"I better get going. Nice to meet you, Emily."

"See ya! Have fun rafting."

Abby left the bathroom and headed into the shop to find the rest of her family.

As the Carters pulled out of the service station, the kids were busy eating their ice cream cones and Marjorie was carefully navigating her coffee into a cup holder. Hank drove a big left-hand arc so he could rejoin the highway

Making this maneuver, he made eye contact with a man sitting in the white van beside the propane tanks. Hank looked at him just long enough to determine that the guy in the van was not going to back out right in front of him. The driver looked a bit creepy to Hank, with his bright orange baseball cap and long sideburns, and pointed goatee. *Definitely not a tourist,* thought Hank, *must be a local yokel.*

As he passed by the rear of the van, he got a flash of sunlight in his face. The bright sun had reflected from some covering on the two rear-door windows.

What kind of asshole puts reflective foil on a car window? Hank thought to himself. *Shouldn't that be illegal?*

Ten minutes later, the Carter family pulled into a small parking lot by a one-story building on the banks of the Nantahala River. There were inflatable river rafts stacked all over the place, and people loading some onto a trailer not far off.

"This is the place! You guys stay in the Caravan, I'm going to quickly check out the NOC," said Hank.

Hank got out and walked to the Nantahala Outdoor Center's Information Center. Inside, he asked a few questions and grabbed a few pamphlets and maps for the family to read later that night in their campsite. The meeting with their rafting guide was scheduled for ten o'clock the next morning.

Hank returned to the vehicle and continued driving to the west, along Highway 19, the Nantahala Gorge Road.

"So, did you get directions to the campsite?" asked Marjorie.

"Yeah, but let's get something to eat before we go."

"Yeah, I'm hungry!" added Nick.

"You're always hungry! But yeah, let's go eat!. According to this map, there's a place called 'Relia's Garden', the staff at the NOC said that it's really great," said Hank.

"Here, Marj, take a look at this map of the Gorge. You see the far left, where the river turns sharply? That's the 'put-in' site. Our campsite is a few miles past that. And you see here, just past where we are here at the NOC? You see 'Relia's Garden'?"

"Oh yeah, I remember seeing that place online. They have organic food on the menu," said Marjorie.

"Organic? What about hamburgers?" asked Nick.

"Oh, I'm sure they'll have food for you hungry carnivores. It's supposed to be just across that little bridge. Eyes on the road, Hank." said Marjorie, decisively.

The four of them were well into their meals and Nick was asking if he could order another burger.

"Let's save some of that appetite for dinner, shall we, champ?" said Hank. Then he made eye contact with the waitress. "Excuse me. Can you please tell us where the Brookside Campground is?"

"Sure. It's about five or six miles west along the Gorge, just before you get to Topton. That's about two miles past the top 'put in'. Are you camping at Brookside tonight?"

"Yeah. But we forgot a few of things at home. Where's a good place to get a few groceries?" asked Marjorie.

"Oh, Mason's in Topton is pretty good, and they have firewood there. You'll also pass a couple of smaller stores along the Gorge, but the one in Topton has better prices."

"Thanks. By the way, the food was great! I'm surprised to find such a great restaurant out here in the boonies. Are most of your customers tourists like us?"

"Boonies? There's actually quite a few permanent residents out here, so we have steady business year round. By the way, we grew all that organic food you just ate," said the waitress attempting a slight resemblance of a smile.

The Carters resumed their drive along the Nantahala Gorge Road.

"What's the name of the campsite we're looking for?"

"Brookside. It's just before Topton," said Hank.

"Oh, I see it," said Marjorie, looking at the pamphlet Hank had picked up at the NOC. "We've got a ways to go, at least another five miles."

As they drove along the Nantahala Gorge Road, Marjorie read off the sites of interest.

"And that's the place we'll take our raft out of the river tomorrow, the take-out point" she said.

"What if we forget to stop?" asked Abby.

"Then we'll get into some trouble, because there are more serious Level Three rapids farther down the river. But don't worry, Rob, our guide, knows what he's doing. He'll make sure we don't go over any waterfalls!" said Hank with authority.

After finding their campsite and unhooking their pop-up tent trailer, they settled in to set up the trailer.

"Marj, it's getting late. Why don't you and Abby go to that grocery store in Topton while Nick and I set up the tent?"

"Sure. But get a good fire going, and throw those potatoes in as soon as you have enough coals. I want them to cook for a good 20 minutes before we put the steaks on."

"So what do we actually need from the store?" asked Hank.

"The one critical thing we forgot was marshmallows, and maybe some extra wine and cream for coffee."

"And don't forget the cocoa!" said Nick.

"Oh yeah, and hot chocolate," said Marj.

"That's not too bad. Last trip we forgot a lot more than that. We're getting better at this camping thing," Hank commented.

"Yeah, Dad. And we'll get even better after we do that orientation thing!" Abby said enthusiastically.

"You're such a little tom-boy, aren't you?" said Marjorie.

Two hours later, after the Carters had enjoyed steak, mashed potatoes and corn-on-the-cob, the sun had disappeared behind the mountains and it was rapidly getting dark.

"Go easy on the wine, Hank," said Marjorie.

"Why? You got some plans for tonight?" Hank asked, mischievously.

"Oh, I was thinking we stay up late, watching the stars. It's nice and warm tonight, not too many mosquitoes. Who knows what could happen."

"We hear you, Mom! Can't you keep your hands off each other? Come on, it's just a little tent! That's disgusting!" said Nick.

While Marjorie pretended not to hear her fourteen year old son's comments, Hank was busy looking around for a suitable place to set out a sleeping bag so that he and Marjorie could make love under the stars.

Marjorie enjoyed her glass of wine while she watched the fire and Hank busied himself moving branches and debris from a spot he had found that was far enough from the campsite to be private, yet not too far. The red heat of the fire, the wine, the fresh air and the wonderful day they had had in the outdoors had put Marjorie into a very contented frame of mind. She started to think about doing something special for Hank that she normally would not do. *Naughty girl!* she thought, smiling to herself in anticipation.

6

DAY OF

Hank and Marjorie had been up late, cuddling in their double-zipped sleeping bag and talking about the future as they both stared up at the stars like a couple of teenagers. They had eventually climbed into their bed on one wing of their pop-up trailer. Abby had the other wing while Nick had the bed made up out of the table.

The adults finally woke up at about nine o'clock to the sounds of wood chopping and their kids talking outside.

"No, we can't start the fire. Mom and Dad aren't up yet."

"Sure we can. This is a *campground*, you are *allowed* to have a fire in a fire pit. Besides, Mom and Dad were up late making out so they'll be really happy if we serve them breakfast in bed. Let's start the fire, and make pancakes!"

Doubtful, but keen on the idea of impressing their parents, Nick got on board. He had been chopping firewood into kindling, and had everything ready to start a fire, but had been waiting for his Dad to get up and be impressed with his survival skills. "OK, Abby, but how are we going to start the fire?"

Smiling mischievously, Abby said, "I'll take care of that!" She flicked the lighter, and lit some paper she had placed in the steel-ringed fire-pit.

"Where'd you get that? You're not supposed to have a lighter. Do you smoke or something?"

"No, smoking is for *Looozers*, like *your* buddies. Dad knows I have this lighter, I used it with him when we burned those leaves and twigs in the back yard last spring. Always be prepared, that's my motto!" she said, putting the lighter back into the pocket of her cut-off shorts.

"What else you got in there?" asked Nick, with a touch of envy.

"I've got this little compass, and a folding knife from Grandpa. But Dad doesn't know about the knife yet," said Abby, showing Nick her contraband.

"You better tell him, or I will," said Nick.

"Sure thing, *Tattle Tale!*"

After squabbling over how to build up the fire, over how to stir the pancake mix, over whether to set the picnic table or serve their parents in the trailer, and over who would take credit for their great idea, the two kids presented a unified front when their Mom and Dad got up and climbed down out of the tent-trailer.

"Mom, Dad! We made you breakfast. Come on and sit down at the table," said Nick as Abby put a cloth in her hand to protect herself from the heat as she took a soot-blackened kettle from the grill over the fire.

"And here's your coffee, twigs and all!" she said.

"What was all that squabbling we heard?"

"Squabbling? We weren't squabbling, Mom. That must have been the squirrels," said Abby.

"Well, the squirrels have outdone themselves. These pancakes look great!"

"Thanks, Dad," said Nick. "So what's the plan for the day? We're going on the river, right?"

"Yeah. First we have to drive back to the Outdoor Center to meet up with Rob, our rafting guide. Then we come back to the 'put-in' site. Take a look here, on the map." Hank spread the pamphlet out on the table.

"So our campsite is here, right? - at Brookside Campground? So we'll go past the put-in site here, near this Wayah Rd? Then we'll actually follow our rafting route, around this corner?" asked Nick, the budding map expert.

Hank looked at the spot where Nick had his finger, "Yeah. That Wayah Road goes all the way up to the headwaters of Nantahala River, by the way. They say there are some great little waterfalls up there, and the river is less powerful so you can swim in some of the pools under those falls. We'll check it out later. Anyhow, from where we are now, if you sit on the right side of the van, you'll be able to get a real good look at the route. Try to keep your eyes out for large boulders and rapids, and think about how we'll have to paddle hard to pull away from the dangerous ones, kind of like a route reconnaissance," said Hank.

"What's this 'bikeway' that starts up here, near the put-in, and goes along on the opposite side of the river from the road?" asked Nick.

"That's closed. The guy at the Outdoor Center told me that it got flooded in those heavy rains last month. There's like six inches of mud all along the bikeway in the low areas up at this end of the gorge. He said he tried to walk it to assess the damage but he got so mired in goopy mud that he couldn't walk more than about ten feet before he gave up. Too bad, 'cause he said it's a wonderful ride. It goes all along the Gorge. But we can ride the part of it farther east, near the Outdoor Center. We just can't ride it all the way from our campsite."

"But if it was clear, we could?" asked Nick.

"I suppose. Maybe we'll come back and do this again next year, and try some of the more challenging river rafting routes, higher up-river, towards the dam."

"Sure, Dad. As long as we don't drown here or something," said Nick.

As they drove along Highway 19 to the NOC, the kids and Marjorie tried to assess the river route along the way. They got increasingly excited but also a little worried about some of the more dramatic rocks and rapids, like 'Patton's Run' and 'Pyramid Rock'.

"I can see why we need to wear helmets!" said Abby. You could really clunk your head on some of those rocks. But our raft is made of rubber, right Dad? So it won't break up if it hits something?"

"Yeah, it's a big soft rubber raft. It'll bounce up and down on the waves so we have to be strapped in hard and hang on. If you fall in, you just ride along in the water with your life-jacket, and swim to the right side. All of the take-out points are on the right. – Look, there's one now! You see that little access trail, just below that bridge?"

Hank inquired, as the highway he had taken his attention from crossed the Nantahala River to the south bank of the Gorge, at Ferebee Park. "So if you get into trouble, this is where you can get out of the river. Understand?"

"Yes, Dad. And we could just walk back to our car, it's only what, a mile or so?"

"Actually, it's more like five miles to this point. No, if you get separated and get out on your own, you just stay put at the take-out site until I get there. That's like a rally point, everybody."

By the time they pulled into the small parking lot at the Nantahala Outdoor Center's Information Center for the second time in as many days, they were very excited about the rafting adventure to come. But they had arrived twenty minutes early for their meeting with their guide, so they walked across the highway to stand by the guard rail and take some pictures of the river.

There were a number of rafts coming down from the left, and a few people could be seen just below them on the right, getting out of their rafts on the shoreline closest to them.

"That must be the lower take-out," said Hank.

"Yeah, it is, at least, according to this pamphlet."

"Where'd you get that, Nick?" asked Abby.

"There's a bunch of them back where we parked, over there," he pointed.

Just then there was a shriek of tires that startled the Carters. They all looked to their right just in time to see that a silver pick-up truck loaded with equipment had slammed on the brakes and just missed T-boning a white Econoline Van. The van swerved around the pick-up truck, with the right wheel nearly lifting off the ground.

As the van passed by, the Carters stared at the driver who was wearing an orange baseball cap. He had a crazed, panicked look on his face that somehow seemed to have nothing at all to do with his near-miss with the pick-up truck.

The van accelerated along the highway to the south-west, while the silver pick-up turned right and headed north-east along the Nantahala Gorge Road. Hank noticed some tin foil covered windows . It seemed to ring a bell, but he could not recall why.

Half an hour later, after having met with their guide Rob, only to be told that they had to go back up the highway to the put-in, where everybody would link up, the family had driven up and down the gorge a few times. They were really starting to know the river better, if not as intimately as they would during their actual rafting run.

They had been parked in the oval-shaped parking lot for the last thirty minutes, but still had not seen anybody from Dickenson's Rafting. Rob should have been there already, with the rafts. The Carters watched in envy as other rafting parties were taking their rafts off the trailers and being given their paddles and life jackets.

"Are you sure we're in the right place, Dad?" asked Nick.

"I think so. This looks like the put-in site, doesn't it?"

"Yeah, but didn't Rob say something about power lines?"

"Yes, he did, didn't he?" said Hank.

"Yeah, he said park under the power lines, in the gravel parking lot – and this one's paved," said Marjorie.

"He did say it was on Wayah Road, right?"

"Yes, Dad. Buy maybe he meant a little farther down the road. Look down that way, aren't those power lines?" said Nick.

Hank looked down the road. He could tell that it was a gravel road by the dust being thrown up by a white van driving down the road. Then he noticed what looked like a series of power lines all feeding into some sort of electrical infrastructure. So the family got back into their

Caravan and drove the few hundred yards towards the electrical substation, traversing a short bridge over a spillway. Just beyond that, they found Rob Dickenson waiting with a trailer loaded with rafts in the gravel parking lot.

"Sorry we're late! We were parked back at that other parking lot," said Hank.

"Don't worry, the other family will be a few more minutes. There's some sort of police check-stop going on near the Rafting Centre, slowing up traffic. They'll be at least another twenty minutes."

"That's a relief. Thought we'd missed the launch!"

"Not at all. But while we wait, let's take the rafts off the trailer and carry them to the put-in," said Rob.

Ten minutes later they had moved the two rafts to a sandy area next to the Nantahala River, piled their paddles nearby, and even put on their life jackets and helmets.

They hung around at the parking lot. Very soon, Abby got restless and wandered down to the river. When she got to the shoreline, she picked some stones out of the sand, and threw a few out over the water. Then she got creative, and picked up one of the paddles and began hitting stones like she was wielding a baseball bat.

One of her stones took a strange vector, and flew off ninety degrees from where she intended. It struck a tree and ricocheted towards a white van parked under some trees on a dirt road to her right. She had not noticed the vehicle when she first arrived, but she could see at least one person in the vehicle, wearing a bright orange baseball cap.

Abby cringed when she realized that the stone was flying towards the vehicle. PING! The stone hit the side of the van.

Abby stood petrified when the door opened and a man got out.

Back in the parking lot, the Carters and Rob were gathered around the silver minivan that had just arrived. The father of the family was excitedly telling everybody about the police check-stop.

"They're looking for a missing girl! She disappeared yesterday from the gas-station at Great Smoky."

"So why the road-block today?" asked Marjorie.

"They're just showing the girl's photograph to everybody, checking cars and asking people to keep their eyes open."

"Wow, that's terrible. What are the police saying?"

"They didn't tell us much, but they think she may have been abducted. She disappeared after going to the bathroom, and the family never left the gas station."

Thinking about their travels the day before, Hank asked: "What time of day, did they say?"

"It was later on, they said, sometime after five."

"That's about the same time we got gas there! What did the girl look like?" asked Hank, looking around at his family. "Hey, where's Abby?"

"She's..." started Marjorie. "Where is she?"

For the next five minutes the Carters searched the parking lot and raft put-in area for Abby, with that low-level feeling of panic you have when you are worried but still believe that the person you are looking for will be located quickly.

They spent a lot of time looking around by the river's edge for any sign that she had gone into the water. Then Hank went back to the parking lot for another sweep. When he saw a white van heading back down Wayah

Road towards Highway 19, he felt his heart drop into his stomach.

He recognized the van and the foiled rear windows. It was the same one he had seen the day before, at the gas station where the young girl had gone missing.

"Marj! Nick! Get in the van!" Hank shouted down towards the river. "HURRY!"

Marjorie and Nick didn't hear him because of the noise from the river. Hank finally got their attention by running down to the river.

"What are you doing? Why are we leaving! Did you see Abby?" asked Marjorie, urgently.

"That white van! I saw it yesterday. It's the kidnappers!"

"What van? I don't see any van", said Marjorie. "THEY JUST LEFT! THEY MIGHT HAVE ABBY!"

In hot pursuit, the Carters reached Highway 19, and Hank looked to his right, and saw nothing. So he turned left, towards Topton, and put his foot to the floor. Marjorie and Nick were silent, terrified as much by Abby's disappearance as by the unfamiliar sight of a wide-eyed Hank Carter losing his mind to grief.

Marj and Nick instinctively held on for dear life.

7

CALM DOWN

Things had become very heated, very quickly. Not only was Hank Carter losing his composure, but the police themselves were having a hard time. They now had two different crime scenes to manage, and the clock was ticking.

"Look, I don't care about who's in charge. We just need to lock this entire region down. That's going to take manpower. Terry, until things are up and running in Asheville and we get more support from Jackson and Haywood Counties, we'll have to take some steps right away with the manpower we have."

"Agreed, but I can't have you in charge of my men, it's just not done that way," said the grumpy old Sheriff from the Graham County.

"But I don't have enough manpower, and this is a Swain County operation. So under the authority I have as Swain County Sheriff, *police force of jurisdiction,* I am invoking the mutual aid agreement that your mayor signed off on just last month. Terry, under that agreement, you and your men will have to take direction from me, until we are all put under command from Asheville. Sorry, but that is what you have to accept."

"I don't like this. It's not supposed to evolve in this loosy-goosy way out in the field, Theo."

Taking Terry Elliott by the elbow, Theo Clarkson also motioned for the Sheriffs from Macon and Cherokee Counties to move aside with them. The head ranger from the North Carolina Wildlife Resource Commission also joined them, without being invited. He was used to being ignored by the Sheriffs, but had good relations with Clarkson, who he dealt with on a daily basis on issues related to tourists up and down the Nantahala Gorge.

When the Ranger and four of the eight different Sheriffs with a stake in the Nantahala National Forest Region were separate from the crowd, Clarkson gave his own deputy a look and a nod that clearly said: *give us some space, keep everybody off our backs for a minute.*

Standing by a picnic table, Sheriff Clarkson spread out a map, placing large stones on the corners to secure it as the people under his temporary command gathered around him.

"Look, Terry, by the time we get this up and running, the Feds will take over. It looks like it's already crossed state lines. At least if we work well together right now, and lock this entire park down, we may just keep this thing from getting completely taken away from us."

Impressed by the respectful way he was being treated by his compatriot, the Graham County Sheriff relented. "OK, Theo, I'm with you. How do you want my men to deploy?"

The Ranger and the Sheriffs from Macon and Cherokee Counties nodded in consensus.

Referring to the map on the table, Theo Clarkson got into the details: "OK. We'll keep it simple. We'll divide the region into four pieces. Most of it is in Swain County, so I want one or two cars from each of you to work with my men. We'll take care of everything from Topton to Bryson City. Albie, you set up roadblocks in Macon County on Highway 28, closer to Franklin than to Lauada, where that first abduction took place. Terry, you guys from Graham County take the Fontana Lake stretch of Highway 28, and all the tracks and roads into Graham county as far west as Andrews. Mike, you sew up the roads from Topton to Andrews and whatever you think needs covering into Cherokee County. What does that leave open?"

"Well, Theo, I can send two cars out from Kyle towards the county line and Otter Creek Road, maybe put someone on Wayah Road, but there's way too many back roads coming down from Fairview. You'll have to handle those yourself."

"Agreed, Albie. Send me those two cars you owe me to patrol on Wayah Road until I get that area sewn up."

Sheriff Albie Singer from Macon County nodded. "I'll put Sergeant Fraser in charge of that sector, and throw three cars at it right away. Fraser knows that area like the back of his hand."

"Great, thanks." Turning to address all the men assembled around him, he raised his voice a notch, and summarized. "So guys, you know the drill, get on with it. I'll back-brief the guys in the Forest Service Headquarters in Asheville, and deal with the jurisdictional issues from the command post I'm setting up at Relia's. As long as we all agree, let's shut this place down. I want the license plate of every vehicle you let out of this region," he indicated with a circular sweep of his hand over the map, making an oval shaped ring around the stretch of the Nantahala River, from Topton to Bryson City, "and detain anybody, and I mean *anybody*, who seems to be hiding anything. He's gone after two girls in twenty-four hours, so he's operating from somewhere around here. We have to be thorough and find these lost children." Clarkson then added, "I don't give a flying F how you do it. Leave the paperwork behind until those innocent kids are safely at home with their parents."

Just as the various Sheriffs headed to their vehicles to pass instructions back to their units, a grey and black SUV pulled up beside Sheriff Clarkson's black patrol car. An immaculately dressed member of the NC State Highway Patrol stepped out of the passenger seat and looked around, sizing up the chaos.

"Officer, which county are you here from?" a reporter shouted from behind the line, clearly addressing the Highway Patrol member who had been driving the vehicle.

The driver of the vehicle looked at the reporter in amusement, "That would be 'Trooper', Ma'am. We're the North Carolina Department of Crime Control and Public Safety, Ma'am. You can contact our public affairs office in Raleigh for more information about the North Carolina

State Highway Patrol." He smiled at the reporter as he scanned the area.

A more astute observer would have noticed the difference between the Trooper's hat-badge, a silver diamond, and that of his more senior passenger's golden diamond, or the golden oak leaf clusters on the man's shoulders. However, the paramilitary rank structure of the Highway Patrol was confusing to some of the tourists in the crowd, who did not know the history of the North Carolina Highway Patrol.

While the Trooper stood his ground near the crowd-control line, it took just a few seconds for those in the know to recognize who was in the zone. He approached Sheriff Clarkson, who stopped what he was doing.

"You must be Major Tyler, from Raleigh, right?"

"That's correct. Sorry I couldn't be here sooner, but I had to check in on Captain Walker in district G6 on the way over."

The two men shook hands in mutual respect.

"I just got off the phone with Captain Walker. He said that the revised AMBER Alert had gone out within ten minutes of our request and that he has two Bell-206 helicopters inbound to assist in the search. Thanks. You guys from the Highway Patrol really know how to spin up."

"Hey, it's what we do. This is your operation, but we pride ourselves in ramping up in the supporting role," said the Major from the NC Highway Patrol Headquarters in Raleigh.

"So were you able to come up with enough Troopers?"

"Yeah. It's 'Theo', right?"

"Yes."

"Right. Well, Theo, we were able to force generate two dozen members. They're all inbound to their assigned locations and will blend in with whatever Sheriff's Department personnel they find, but as we agreed on the phone, they will only assist in the management of the AMBER Alert, traffic control and passing information up the line to our North Carolina Centre for Missing Children. That means that I do not have any personnel left to contribute to the manhunt – other than the air support, of course," said Major Tyler.

"Well, that solves a couple of pieces of the puzzle. Thanks for the support. But I'm still not sure how to work with Asheville on that. Do we push info from our units in the field to my dispatcher in Bryson City on the common frequency, or do we pass it all through Asheville and from there over to your District Headquarters in Bryson City?"

"That's all fucked up. But I can tell you right from the lips of my Colonel in Raleigh, get on with the manhunt and lock this place down and use your normal chain of command. It's all got to go HQ to HQ. We can't lose the big picture by changing procedures on all of our personnel."

"That's what I was hoping to hear. Even though we've done this sort of thing before, albeit on a much smaller scale, there are always the same jurisdictional issues and people running around like chickens with their heads cut off. We all need to calm down, do our jobs, and get a grip."

"Amen to that."

"What about the State Bureau?" asked Clarkson.

"The State Bureau of Idiots?"

"Come on. I have some friends there."

"Me too. But the entire organization is a waste of time, if you ask me. Whenever we get one of these things that's big enough to warrant yet another layer on the cake, it quickly goes federal and our SBI only comes back into it when there is enough evidence for the DAs to lay charges."

"That's not the way we see it from down here. We put in our request for their assistance, and they're sending a team over from Wake County to assist."

"Assist how?"

"Their Special Ops Division is getting more air support for the search, for one. That's much needed. And they're also mobilizing their mobile crime lab from Asheville to process any time-sensitive evidence right here in the field. They're going to set up at a local restaurant, just across that bridge over there."

"OK. I'll grant that the SBI can be of help, and I know some of their field agents are first rate, but I guess my grief with them is that their DAs sometimes get too concerned with pleasing the Governor than with making sure they have their shit together – you know how many times some jerk gets off because of a technicality the SBI should have had covered?"

"You're talking about the murder case against that Seiprecht character, over in Franklin?"

"For one, yeah," said Tyler.

"Well, it may not be as simple as it looks, in that case. One of the senior Deputies from Macon County told me that Seiprecht really isn't that bad of a guy. He's mentally screwed up, from his time in Iraq, but he's basically just a loser who found himself in the wrong place at the wrong time. He says that 'Sex Offender' rap was overdone, more like a guy not knowing the girl he picked up was under age or something, and that he had nothing to do with that Freeman murder, according to Sergeant Fraser, anyhow.

"Well, we can debate this stuff some other time, Sheriff, you've got an investigation to run, and I see there's a long line of people you need to deal with. Where do you want me to set up my CP?"

"Why not over at Relia's Garden with your SBI pals?"

"Sure. Makes sense. I'll play nice with them, don't worry about that. Is that the restaurant across the bridge?"

"Yeah. I'll come and look for you there in a half hour or so. That's also where I'm operating from. Not much space around here. When the FBI gets here, they'll have to set up in the quarry farther back."

"FBI? Why are they into this already, I would have thought this would stay a State issue."

"Didn't you hear about the Gorton girl?" asked Theo.

"No. What?"

"There's been a third abduction, just over state lines on highway 71, about seven miles into Tennessee. A 12-year old red-headed girl, Elisa Gorton, has gone missing from the Chimneys Campground. It's the same MO as the Emily Harper case. So the FBI are coming in. We still don't know if or when they'll federalize the entire operation, so I'm operating under the assumption that even if they do, it won't change the task before us."

"I see, but it will mean that all those federal resources will be brought to bear on this search as well. That's a double-edged sword, Sheriff." Looking up at the steep mountains along the gorge, Major Tyler continued. "When things get to that big of a scale, things can go wrong. Who's handing the airspace?"

"Airspace? The pilots, I guess. What are you thinking?"

"I'm thinking that we need to manage this more like a military operation, so that the lines of command and control are understood by all, but also so that the management of the airspace and the ground search are handled appropriately and suit the scale of the operation."

"I think you're going where I have not even had a chance to consider, so go on, Major."

"Well, as you know, we share our Headquarters in Raleigh with the North Carolina National Guard. I think it would make sense for us – for you – to put in a request for airspace and Ground Search and Rescue management. That would bring in the specialized skill sets and communications capabilities needed to manage this thing right."

"Well, that makes sense for the airside, but why Ground Search and Rescue. This is a missing person search, more like a manhunt than SAR."

"Yeah, but what about that Carter girl? She could have just fallen into the river. So that gives you a GSAR card to play. Really, Sheriff, that's the best way to get the help you need."

"OK. I'll do the paperwork later. Consider this my request to your Department for Airspace and GSAR management. Will that work for you, Major?"

"You said the magic words!" said the Major from the NC Highway Patrol. "I'll get right on it. I'm heading over to that restaurant now. Good luck herding the kittens, Sheriff!"

"Yeah, same to you, Major. Just tell one of my boys who you are and he'll set you up with some maps and brief you on the disposition of personnel and the latest reports."

The Carters had been held back with the rest of the crowd, watching the group of Sheriffs and other law enforcement types all just standing around talking. It looked to Hank Carter that they were working out jurisdictional issues, and that this was wasting valuable time. As frustrated as he was to see this, he understood that this was not the Air Force, where there was always a clear chain of command and the overriding principle of *operational imperative*. With police forces, you had to work out which force was in charge, who was in a supporting role, what the command and control arrangements were, and only then get into the battle plan.

So when Hank saw the Sheriff's break up, and each head to their own cluster of cruisers, issuing orders to their men standing around and then getting on their radios, he was relieved. Hank had a great deal of respect for other men in uniform, and for police officers in particular. Had he not made it through his pilot training, he would have become a police officer back in his hometown of Grand Forks, North Dakota, where his father had served for his entire career.

"What's happening?" asked Marjorie, as the police cars untangled themselves and began to hit the road.

"They're deploying their forces," said Hank.

"Aren't they already out there? It's been over an hour since we reported Abby missing!" complained Marjorie.

"Oh, they've been out there all this time. They were already out there stopping cars when they issued that

AMBER Alert for the missing girl from that gas station. But now they are ramping up a much larger operation, to help find Abby as well." The words were coming out logically, but Marjorie could tell that Hank was on the edge.

"Well, it looks like they wasted a lot of time. Are you OK, Hank?"

"No. I *can't stand* this standing around, waiting. As much as I understand it, I want to *do* something," Hank said. "If this had been a military operation, they would still be working on the Order of Battle and issuing orders, and nobody would have deployed. Of course, with the Army, they would eventually deploy on a massive scale. But for something like this, the police agencies actually deploy much faster than we could. Overall, I think they are doing a good job getting on with it. But I think there are some holes in their plan."

"Why don't you tell him, that guy who seems to be in charge."

"I'm trying to, Marj, but he's been too busy. Wait a second," Hank said, as he saw Sheriff Clarkson walking his way.

"Sheriff! Sheriff! I need to talk to you!" called out Hank.

Without breaking his stride, the Sheriff looked at Hank with a stone cold expression.

"Mr. Carter, the best thing you could do for you daughter right now is stay out of my way. You can go over to my Command Post, over at Relia's, and wait there. I will talk to you when I can, but I've got a million things to take care of first," he said, without breaking his stride or looking back at Hank when he was done.

Hank was not satisfied, and ducked under the yellow band of POLICE LINE – DO NOT CROSS tape that had been strung upside-down across the area to control the crowd adjacent to the NOC Information Center.

"Sheriff, I am talking to you!" Hank said to the back of the man's hat, as he closed to arms length of the Sheriff.

He never got his hands on him, as two muscular Deputies closed in on Hank and grabbed his arms.

"Mister. You don't want to bother the Sheriff," one of the Deputies said with that articulate but firm tone of voice that law enforcement types often use as a last warning.

"What about the van! Have you found the van, Sheriff?" Hank called after Clarkson, as he was manhandled back to his wife behind the line.

A couple of reporters in the crowd overheard Hank's comment, and knew that he was the father of one of the missing girls.

"What van, Sheriff?" asked a reporter.

As Clarkson waded into the throng of local officials and media, Hank led Marj and Nick back to their minivan, with two deputies following a few steps behind.

As he pulled out and headed for the bridge, he saw that the Sheriff had been as short with the crowd as he had been with Hank. Clarkson was already headed to his cruiser and the crowd were all rushing for their cars.

"Look, Marj, we got out of there just in time. They're all headed to Relia's now as well. At least we'll get there ahead of everybody else!" Hank said, excitedly, accelerating the minivan towards the bridge.

"Look, Hank. I can't take this, and I can tell you're coming unglued. It's too stressful hanging around here, not doing anything. Why don't we just go back to the campsite, and wait there. Maybe Abby's found her way back and we're not there!"

"That's probably a good idea," Hank acknowledged, clearly torn between being close to the investigation and being back at the campsite. His driving was not the smooth, careful driving of an Air Force pilot, but the jerky, stop-and-go driving of a rally-car driver. He was gripping the steering wheel so tightly that his hands were going white. "But I want to see how they're organized, maybe get some names and phone numbers before we go back to the campsite, OK?"

"Why do you need names and numbers? Are you going to pester them, or let them do their jobs?" She regretted her remarks before they left her lips.

"Shut up!" Hank shouted at her in a tone she had never heard before. It was not like Hank to bark at her like that, and it made her afraid that he might even hit her. So she kept silent for the rest of the short drive up to Relia's Garden restaurant.

After quickly dealing with a few local officials and the first of the media to arrive, Sheriff Clarkson had gotten into his cruiser and listened to the reports on the radio, to get a sense of how the deployment was going. When there was a lull in the chatter, he picked up the radio.

While he talked, he kept his eyes moving across the area, as police officers do habitually. He registered that the Carter family were crossing the bridge to Relia's, as he had instructed them to do.

With a ten year old daughter of his own, Theo was sympathetic to the Carters' plight, and committed to himself that he would make time to talk to the man for a few minutes when he got to his CP.

"Swain Dispatch, this is Swain Actual, over."

"Go ahead, Sheriff, over" said Sandy, the dispatcher.

"Be advised that a Major from the Highway Patrol has checked in, and is co-locating his CP with ours, at Relia's. They are going to coordinate the airspace and some GSAR resources, over."

"Say again, GSAR? What's that? over."

"Ground Search and Rescue. They're going to coordinate with the National Guard to help manage the search parties on the ground as well as the airspace. How copy? over."

"Good copy, Sheriff. We've had some inquiries about the airspace, so that will be good news. When you coming over here? There have been a lot of calls for you, and we need you here on a land line, Sheriff, over."

"I'm on my way to Relia's. Has anybody arrived from Asheville yet? over"

"Yup. They're setting up now in your CP, and they're happy with what you've done so far. They're going to let you continue as lead, over"

"That's good news, over."

"Yup. And their Public Affairs girl really knows how to get the reporters in line. She's setting them up for you to make a statement in about 20 minutes, over."

"I don't know if I can be ready that fast, over," said Sheriff Clarkson, as he drove up the driveway to Relia's.

"Don't worry, Sheriff, I've already seen the speaking notes she's prepared for you. You'll do fine, over."

"I'm here at Relia's now. Sheriff out!" he said, as he parked in the handicap parking spot right in front of the restaurant. The expansive gravel parking lot was now chock-full of police vehicles, ambulances, a fire truck, several un-marked cars, and a few TV mobile trucks.

As he walked into what he expected to be a scene of total chaos, Sheriff Clarkson made an effort to bring the images of the three missing girls into the forefront of his mind, just to remind himself of what this activity was all about. Entering the building, he started looking for Mr. Carter while sizing up how the ramping up of the combined Command Posts was coming along.

As Hank jostled the minivan into a parking spot on the shoulder of the road leading into Relia's restaurant, Marjorie considered saying something to try to get Hank to calm down. She thought of appealing to his professionalism as a military officer to get his emotions under control, but was too afraid to say anything.

As she watched Hank walk away from their minivan, she worried what he might do if things did not go well inside. She thought about how it must be for Hank. Not only must it be difficult for him because of his very close bond with Abby, but he had also been so close to stopping that van when she had disappeared. And now there was nothing he could do

Hank entered the restaurant. It had been entirely transformed, to the point that the interior bore only the slightest resemblance to the expansive, rustic restaurant that the family had visited just the day before. Now there were magnetic white-boards mounted on walls, bulletin-boards erected on improvised posts, and computers set out in clusters of three or four on dining room tables that had been pushed together. From the improvised signage hanging over the workstations, Captain Carter was able to glean the basics of how the combined Command Post was being organized.

He was about to find a pen and start taking down names and asking for phone numbers, when he heard footfalls coming up to him from behind, and turned around.

"OK, Mr. Carter, I can give you five minutes now. But after that, I want you to take your family back to your campsite, and wait there. Deputy Craddock will keep you informed, and you will be in the best place to help Abby if she hopefully is only lost, or alternatively gets loose and somehow finds her way to where you are camped. Can you do that for me?"

"Yes, Sheriff. Thanks. And I'm sorry I lost it back there. I'm just," he stammered, mentally shutting down, "I can't......"

The tortured, red-faced expression of anguish and hopelessness on Hank Carter's face was suddenly replaced by the calm, cool, professional visage of Captain Hank "Peanut" Carter, as his military training somehow rose up to out-rank the desperate father.

"Air Power. What are you doing about air power? I can call base operations at Dover, and get some air assets up here. Get me in contact with an operator," Hank ordered, as if the Swain County Sheriff were one of his subordinates.

"We've got that under control. We have two helicopters in the area now, and more on their way soon. We are getting the airspace coordinated by the National Guard, out in Raleigh, and we've got additional resources being generated from a variety of agencies," said Clarkson, making a sweeping gesture across the combined CP.

"Sheriff, I don't mean to tell you how to do your job, but do you have any idea how large this search area is?"

"Listen, mister, I know you're with the Air Force, but just stay out of the way and let us do our job. If we need your help, we'll ask for it!" Despite his concern for the Carter family, Sheriff Clarkson decided that now was not the time for compassion.

"But —"

"Now get out of here before I have you removed from the Park altogether." The Sheriff turned abruptly and walked away from Hank. He did not want the Air Force officer to see the confusion on his face. As confident as he was that he could manage all of the personnel from the four counties surrounding the two crime scenes, and the additional complexities of the State and Federal agencies, he knew that he was out of his league. This thing was going to become a zoo.

Hank stood there, watching Clarkson being swarmed by CP personnel. He was certain that the Sheriff would not give him a third chance, so he turned around and walked out of Relia's. He was just as worked up as he had been when he entered, but he had more confidence in the situation.

I've got to get myself under control, if I'm going to be of any use around here, Hank thought to himself.

Forty-eight hours later the search had been taken over by three successive jurisdictions. Firstly, the North Carolina Forest Police headquarters in Asheville had taken command, making use of the original plan established by the Swain County Sheriff. Secondly, the mobile command post from the North Carolina State Bureau of Investigations had arrived, destroying the lettuce patch in the organic garden on the far side of Relia's in the process. They had agreed to let Swain County continue to be the police agency of jurisdiction, but had declared the investigation to be a major crime, and under the jurisdiction of the North Carolina Attorney General, and therefore the SBI wanted to call the shots.

It was painfully clear to Major Thomas Tyler that there would be no change to how the battle would be fought on the ground, as the SBI did not have the resources to manage such a massive manhunt, nor to handle the interview and processing of so many people in the area of operations. What it was all about was getting their faces into the limelight, to be behind the releases of information, and to take the lion's share of the credit for any good news that could be forthcoming. But he had to admit, their crime lab was staffed with some of the most competent CSI personnel in the region, and could prove to be very useful. He looked forward to speaking to Ginger. She gave it to him straight with no bullshit. She also had minted his underground moniker, 'Major Tom'.

Less than 12 hours later the entire operation was federalized when the body of the missing Gorton girl was found on the North Carolina side of the border, where Highway 71 climbed to the summit over the Beech Flats. Since the abducted girl from Tennessee was found in North Carolina, her body had crossed a state border. Now the FBI could take the whole ball of wax and throw up further complications for the involved jurisdictions.

Her body had been shredded horribly, and dumped over the railing of a scenic look-out, where tourists stopped to take pictures of the panoramic view of the Smoky Mountains.

The tourists who had found her were still in shock, and could not get the image of the poor girl out of their minds. Fortunately for them, the SBI had called in a team of therapists to help with grief counseling.

Tyler had looked in on the witnesses, and saw that the children were responding to the young woman who was consoling them, as her superior spoke with the parents.

After checking the witnesses, Tom Tyler then followed up on the victim. The body of young Elisa Gorton was in a mobile lab, just outside of the CP at Relia's.

Tyler was on good terms with the staff of the SBI Crime Lab, and quietly approached one of the investigators, working at her computer.

"How's it going, Ginger?"

"Back for your thirty-minute update?"

"Just got here. Am I coming over too often?" he asked with a smirk.

"Not at all, 'Major Tom'! Actually, I think you're keeping the CP from others wanting to beat down our door. You timed your visit to perfection."

Tyler smiled inwardly as he heard the moniker that few uttered in his presence but called him behind his back. Ginger was one that dared say it to him on such a personal level.

"Why? Tell Major Tom what you found."

"We've completed the rape kit, the blood work, and the toxicology. I have the coroner's initial report also."

"What did you learn?"

"This is all preliminary, and has to be confirmed by the double-blind, but it appears that she was not sexually assaulted. Actually, she was a virgin. No surprise, as she's just ten years old. She was pre-pubescent, by the way."

Tyler's eyes turned up at that. After all, he was just a major in the highway patrol. Suddenly, the obligations attached to that title brought him to ground as he focused on what Ginger was saying.

"Yeah, but she put up a good fight. She has defensive wounds on her hands, and we recovered some skin from under her nails, so we may get some good DNA from that."

"So how did she die?"

"Multiple trauma. She has numerous internal injuries, a broken hip bone, broken femur, shattered wrists, contusions all over her body, neck broken in two places, and a variety of abrasions on her arms, legs and buttocks."

"Was this from a beating, or what?"

"No. It all happened in a short time-frame, and from the bitumen we found in her abrasions, our preliminary finding is that she died on the road, tumbling, as if from a moving vehicle. We've heard from agents at the scene that they are cutting out pieces of road that may have been surfaces she was abraded on, with measurements and photographs for a virtual reconstruction. But that's what it looks like to me."

"So she was thrown out of a vehicle?"

"That's the great thing," said the SBI Crime Lab technician excitedly, rolling Elisa's body over. "You see this mark on her lower back?"

"Yeah."

"We recovered some paint from it. It's come up as a match for a type of base coat or final coat of paints used commonly in the automotive industry."

"Can you narrow down the make?"

"No. It's used too widely. But it got us going on the shape of that particular wound."

"And?"

"Unless we find a better candidate, it appears to be most consistent with those hoop-shaped levers used as latches on the lower portion of a double-door, like in a van or in a split-door SUV."

"Interesting. Anything else from the blood work?"

"Loads!" We found Trichloromethane in her blood. – I know what you're going to say, the blood method has not been standardized yet. So we did gas chromatography from alveolar air collected onto carbonaceous sorbent, and it confirmed what we got from whole blood extraction. But that's not good enough for the new Director, what with what happened with that guy who was exonerated because of misleading serology reports. So now we need to do as many as three independent forms of confirmatory reports, and highlight any negative findings we get. In this case, there are no negative findings in any of the blood samples. Just to be sure, we tested urine from her bladder, added proteolytic enzyme and did thermal desorption. Bang! Confirmed three ways from Sunday," she said, triumphantly.

"You lost me a long way back. Can you give it to me in English, please?"

"She was chloroformed orally, nose and mouth. So my theory is this. When she was abducted at that campsite, they gassed her, bagged her, and transported her.. Probably fifteen minutes later, she came to and fought her way out of the bag and right out of the vehicle, falling on one of those U-Hoops in the process of getting out the door, landing on the road. She was killed by the road, trying to escape."

"So how did she get into the gully, off the road, where she was eventually found?"

"That's the other part. There are post-mortem bruises on her wrists. She was probably dragged off the road, and tossed over the railing by her killers."

"But if she was killed by road, can the charge be murder? You make a broad assumption that there was more than one person involved. Assuming that is true, give me the rest of your report, Ginger."

"Sure. They could not have known that she was dead. For all we know, she may have been alive for ten or twenty minutes after falling out of the vehicle. So they denied her the chance for medical intervention, at best. And if they had not abducted her, none of this would have happened, so the SBI will definitely recommend indictment on a long list of charges. And unplanned developments like this, with the girl falling out of the vehicle, usually generates lots of evidence. We'll get these guys," she said, confidently.

"Guys? How do we know there were two, and both male? For that matter, what if there were three perps?"

"Just stands to reason, one person had to be driving the vehicle, because it was in motion at the time. There must have been at least one other accomplice, and that's the un-sub we may have DNA from, from under her nails. By the way, your perp will have two or three deep gouges somewhere on his body."

Ginger fluttered her eyelashes at her 'Major Tom'.

Taking a print-out of the lab's preliminary report and a copy of the coroner's initial findings back to the CP to share with the other agencies, Thomas Tyler was optimistic that they may have just received a considerable break in the case. He thought to himself – *that's 'my Ginger'.*

8

SEARCHING

With one girl now dead, and two other girls still missing, the national and international media were giving the search continuous coverage. It seemed as if the stream of resources pouring into the search area was endless.

In addition to perhaps five hundred county, state and federal personnel, over three hundred civilian volunteer searchers had been organized by the various overlapping police and federal jurisdictions involved. They were managed by a highly efficient Ground Search and Rescue headquarters which had been stood up in a complex of modular tents erected by the North Carolina National Guard on the tennis courts of the Nantahala Village Resort, just a stone's throw from the combined CP in Relia's restaurant.

Captain Alex Parisienne, the GSAR Search Master from the National Guard had kicked a national television network out of the spot but also helped the media to establish a new broadcast site near a small gravel quarry just a short distance behind the Nantahala Resort Center.

The GSAR teams were deployed to conduct searches in expanding patterns focused on the three "Last Known Points", or LKPs. The GSAR team and volunteer augmenters from Tennessee assigned to search the Chimneys Campground off US Route 441 had been released once the Gorton girl had been found up at the summit just inside North Carolina. There were still a dozen agents crawling over the area where the Gorton family had been camping, gathering evidence and interviewing potential witnesses, but that was not a concern for Captain Parisienne.

He was now focused on finding the Carter girl, somewhere along the Nantahala gorge, and the missing Harper girl, who went missing from the gas station near Bryson city.

It did not matter to the GSAR Team Leader that the two girls may have been abducted. To him, finding any sign of them, whether alive or dead, whether by natural or human cause, was a mechanical task of personnel management.

With his Aerospace Control cell managing the specially designated 'Smoky Mountain Search' airspace, comprised of 400,000 acres in a twenty-five mile by twenty-five mile box centered on a south-west to north-east line from Andrews to Bryson City, Alex was certain that he had enough resources in the air.

Some of the police helicopters involved were equipped with electro-optical infra-red and real-time digital image streaming capabilities. This made the police helicopters even more useful than the military helicopters and fixed wing aircraft he had stacked at higher altitudes. But he was using all possible resources to ensure full coverage and frequent revisit time to the various search patterns he had tasked to the flying units. However he relied most on the police services equipment which gave him a much better real-time air and ground picture, displayed on the various computer and television screens set up in the search headquarters.

On the ground, he had a combination of experienced and qualified GSAR personnel from civilian and law enforcement rescue teams, as well as Combat Search and Rescue personnel from his National Guard unit in Raleigh.

That the military CSAR personnel were also armed had been an issue for some of the police and Sheriff's departments. However his Base Commander had explained to the Governor that, "When you call out the National Guard, what you get is armed soldiers, not civilians".

Having the civilians in the mix was actually very good, from Alex's perspective. Many of them had local knowledge that really helped with communications and with building up the situational awareness of the unfamiliar searchers and those coordinating the search effort, like himself.

The mix was aided by a contingent of first responders from a variety of Emergency Medical Services paramedics and firefighters. They had proven very helpful in rescuing some unfortunates who had become injured or needed rescue themselves from some of the more dangerous terrain that they had attempted to search.

As in any large scale operation, reflected Alex, just keeping the aircraft and ground searchers safe, hydrated and fed was a job in itself.

But the most satisfying part was when the search object was found, and that was his focus as Search Master.

For the Harper girl, in addition to continuous air searches for anything moving that had not been identified and approved by the police forces, Parisienne deployed teams to search 400 yards on both sides of highway 28, from highway 19 all the way to the Franklin airport, and east and west on highway 19 for ten miles. But from what he had learned of the circumstances of the disappearance of the Harper girl, he was not expecting to find anything.

As much as it went against his training to think in this way, Alex had the most hope for finding the Carter girl. He had water-born teams scouring the river, from two miles above the top 'put-in' point, where she had gone missing, all the way along the Nantahala Gorge to the top of the Nantahala Falls. He had teams below the falls as well, all the way to the Almond Boat and RV Park where the river passed Highway 28.

The boaters helping with the searches along that stretch of deep, wide water leading into Fontana Lake had been a thorn in his side. To Alex, many of them were well-meaning volunteers, but they had no idea how to do a shoreline crawl, nor were they particularly accurate in sticking to their assigned area. A few of them were yahoos, roaring up and down the search area making trouble for those more dedicated to their assignment..

The terrain from one end of the Carter search zone, as he had marked it on the Master Search Map, had been broken down into a variety of sub-sectors. It was very challenging terrain, encompassing over two hundred square miles, and that was only the initial search area.

As the teams completed their tasks, and the Search Master's staff marked them as completed on the master map, Alex built out a secondary search area going as far as twenty miles to either side of the Nantahala River.

This is where the troubles began. His personnel, sincerely trying to find the missing girls, were not respecting the property rights of the owners of the many cabins and other structures in the area.

They had been instructed to leave the private property to the police to check out, but in many cases searchers had surprised people enjoying their property, and terrified more than a few civilians in the process.

What's more, worried Alex, the large number of people involved in planning and managing the operation – not all of them from the National Guard – meant that there was absolutely zero operational security. *If the bad guys wanted to, they could simply infiltrate the search teams, perhaps as volunteers, and be briefed in on the search patterns, tasks and timings*, he thought to himself with frustration.

He gave his head a shake, and carried on with doing the job he was trained to do as Search Master – find the missing girls. *Leave the crime-fighting to the Law Enforcement Officers. The LEOs' will catch the creep(s).*

The first days had been chaotic, with over a dozen articles of clothing found along the banks of the river. Each article had to be checked against photographs taken hours before Abby went missing. Nothing matched.

Then the heavy rains came on the third day. Searching the river became much more dangerous, and a number of participants slipped and fell on wet rocks, breaking more than a few arms and legs in the process. After that period of time, their spirits were breaking also.

To Alex, the heavy rain marked the end of a promising search phase and started the gradual decline of hope. He knew if the lost children were not found within the first forty-eight to seventy-two hours, there was little hope of finding them alive, if at all. It would eventually become a recovery search, looking for bodies, not survivors.

The heavy rains of the third night marked a change in the field reports. There was a huge reduction in the number of observations. The reports started to reflect more and more wishful thinking, like one from the Queen's Creek Lake area, where an excited searcher reported hearing singing. An EOIR equipped helicopter was placed on that location, followed by a search team that only discovered that the searcher believed the reported singing had been a figment of her imagination.

Another report from the areas close to where Abby Carter went missing drew attention to tracks leading out of a muddy area beside a bicycle trail into the rocks in the hillside above. However, the searchers became hopelessly mired in the muck. They had been careful to watch for any tracks leading into the muddy area, from both ends of the bike trail, but found no tracks other than their own. They had not been able to confirm if the originally reported tracks had ever existed, as they had made such a mess of the area.

Parisienne put it down to yet another false positive, and filed the report. He then generated yet another, larger grid, expanding the search area yet again.

The normally congested roads of the Nantahala Gorge were now veritable parking lots, with all manner of police and emergency response vehicles, media trailers, and even a contingent of USAF. Captain Hank Carter had advised his Wing Commander, who had organized a company from the Dobson Air Force Base survival school to blend in with the GSAR staff from the National Guard.

While helicopters searched the rivers and valleys day and night, air support from Georgia, Tennessee and North Carolina were aided by C130 Hercules aircraft dropping extremely powerful parachute-flares that illuminated the search area,

To the uninformed, the area appeared more like a war zone than the peaceful parkland it normally was.

For the Carters, essentially held captive in the Brookside Campground awaiting news, it was pure and unadulterated hell. They no longer pestered the powers that be for any information. It was obvious to them that a great many people were doing everything they could to find their missing daughter and the young girl missing from the gas station. They tried not to think about the implications coming from the media about the Tennessee girl found dead, assuring themselves that it must not be connected with Abby's disappearance. But both Hank and Marjorie knew that they were fooling themselves. It was just too much of a coincidence, with three girls all about the same age going missing in such a short timeframe.

Pastor Sullivan, from the Carter's parish near the airbase in Marietta, arrived on the second day in a HMVW, driven by a Military Police sergeant. Knowing that Hank could not sit idly by, nor could he leave the area, Pastor Sullivan and Sergeant Fitzpatrick came through. They somehow arranged for a section of mod tent and a satellite uplink at the Brookside campsite. Ostensibly to support the coordination of military volunteers, it actually was to give Hank a sense of purpose. Pastor Sullivan observed Hank and knew he was watching a train wreck in slow motion.

He had seen it before, in his ministering to the needs of families from the various units located at Dobson Air Force base. Many of the situations were those that any pastor could deal with, but there were also unique problems faced by military personnel returning from deployments to war zones and disaster areas like Iraq, Myanmar and Haiti. In some cases, he dealt with Post Traumatic Stress Disorder, family chaos, and at times significant personality changes.

Thinking about Iraq, Pastor Sullivan had a moment of inspiration. He headed to his tent to find his cell phone. As he waited for his call to be answered, he felt sure that the man on the other end would take an interest in Captain Carter and his family.

9

ERRATIC BEHAVIOR

The interview had gone on for over four hours before Hank caught on to what was really happening.

"Look, I've told you this all again and again."

"Just go through it again for me, to make sure I have it right," said the investigator. "Now, tell me again, when was the last time you crossed state lines into Tennessee?"

"Why do you keep asking me that? I haven't been in Tennessee in like three years. Well, I've been there a few weeks ago, but that was in a Hercules aircraft."

"So which is it, three years or a few weeks ago? You're being very inconsistent on that point."

"Look, Special Agent Zinck, is it? I'm sick of this shit. I need to be out there looking for Abby, or be in a place she can find me. She's out there someplace, all alone.

Or she is in some kind of danger. She is a very smart kid, you know, and if there's a way to get free and run for it, she'll do it. So I have to be out there to find her when she does."

"Why do you think she has come to harm. Have you harmed her?"

"Are you out of your fucking mind! What is wrong with you people?"

"We are trying to find out what happened to your daughter, and we need your cooperation in it."

"But I HAVE been cooperating with you. We've gone over it like five times already. What more do you want. And what are you not telling me."

"We –"

"Wait a minute. You're FBI. That means what, you've come and taken over from those locals?"

"You mean the North Carolina Highway Patrol, or the North Carolina State Bureau of Investigation?"

"State FBI? What?"

"State Bureau of Investigation. I know it sounds weird, but North Carolina has this extra level of specialists who handle major crimes like yours."

"Like mine? What, you think I am involved in whatever has happened to my own daughter?"

"That's not what I meant."

"Yes it is. You've been wearing me down like a *suspect*, haven't you?" Hank realized, angrily, but then thought about the bigger picture. "Look, I know that's part of your job, to look at everybody until you figure out who could be involved. And I think that a lot of missing kids turn out to be parental abductions, like in custody battles. But Marj and I are solid, we are not in any kind of problems together. Go ahead and ask her. We are a happy family and we were just out camping and about to go on the river with our guide, and wham! – Abby's gone. But you know all of this. Why aren't you looking for that van I saw? The one that the County Sheriff guy said they had been looking for at that first roadblock, when they put out the AMBER ALERT for that Harper girl? And why are you FBI guys involved?"

The agent broke protocol a bit, and took the pressure off of Hank for a moment. "Look, Captain, you're right, we are just going through the motions to see if you are involved, it's procedure. And even if I don't think you are involved, I will keep on you and all the other persons of interest, including David – er, the guy with the van. But to answer your question, this became our case when the Tennessee State Police reported the particulars of a case they are working on that has a number of parameters that match your case and that of the abduction of the Harper girl earlier in the day."

"That's the girl they found dead today, right? What are the similarities?"

"Yes. Well, age and appearance of the girls, reports of a white van –"

"With some back windows covered in tin foil?" interrupted Hank.

"Yes."

"So what, because it's involving abductions in North Carolina and Tennessee, two different states jurisdictions, that makes it an FBI case?"

"Yeah, that and the scale of the search effort that is now underway. We had to federalize it or it would have become a complete dog's breakfast."

Calmed down slightly now that he was getting some information, Hank became less agitated and more focused.

"You mentioned a name, David? Who is that, the owner of the van?"

"We don't know that. I can't get into it. It was a mistake for me to let that name slip out. Just forget about it, it does not concern you."

Suddenly angry again, Hank lunged at the agent and nearly got hold of his lapel before the agent jerked back and out of reach. "You son of a bitch! If it has anything to do with my daughter, then it *does* concern me!"

Getting up out of his chair and moving towards the door, the agent was clearly flustered by Hank's outburst. "Look, Henry, you would be a lot better off if you just simmer down and let the professionals do their jobs."

"So are we done here, Agent Zinck? Can I go now?" asked Hank, calming down again.

"Yes, we're done, but you've got to pack up and head home. You will be driven back to your campsite by Special Agent Underwood, who will come for you here in a few minutes once I've processed you and cleared you out, and then you've got to pack up and go home to Atlanta."

"Why can't I stay here and wait for news about Abby. Aren't they still searching for her and the other girl?"

"Yes, but it's been almost a week now and this search is costing a fortune. They have covered the search area three ways from Sunday now with nothing found. It's time for us all to move our focus on to the investigation."

"You mean find that van and that David guy, and put the screws on all of the others 'persons of interest?"

Exasperated at having lost control of the interview, Agent Zinck looked meaningfully at Hank. "Something like that Henry, something like that." Special Agent Zinck left Hank alone in the interview room.

In a corner office on another floor at the FBI Resident Agency office in Asheville, the Special Agent-in-Charge from the FBI North Carolina Division office in Charlotte was in a heated discussion with his SAC counterpart up from the Atlanta office. The Assistant Special Agent-in-Charge from the Knoxville office was more of an interested observer in the debate, and not at all worked up.

"Look, I agree with you that Zinck and the other guys here in Asheville have done a good job so far, but here's my concern. Both families are from Atlanta, and three of the suspects are Georgia residents. So even if the crime scene is in your backyard, this file should come down to the Atlanta Division."

"I agree with your logic, Agent Dunbar, but don't you think we should wait until we get a definitive decision from the grown-ups?"

"Fuck, Ashton, you really are a jerk. We are SACs! We are supposed to lead this stuff, and only call on the head office when it gets political or we really are at an impasse. And we haven't even got started yet! It was difficult enough for you to push your SBI guys off of this one, and that's with a murder in Tennessee and two missing children from Georgia! Come on, cut the crap and cut this loose to me. I'll handle any blow-back from the head office," said SAC Dunbar.

"What about you, Agent Williams, do you agree with Dunbar?"

"Yes, I agree, you are a jerk, Ashton," he said, only half jokingly. "Hey, the first victim was mine, but I can see where this is going. The Atlanta office has the best Evidence Response Team, the best lab and one of the better Hostage Rescue Teams. I say we agree here and now, you two SACs and me, the lowly ASAC – And I have my SAC's authority on this one – that we all agree here and now to call this a joint investigation involving all three Divisions, we appoint Special Agent-in-Charge Dunbar here as the lead, and we agree to push any information that we develop right into his office, and give him any support that he asks for. Then we put a ribbon on it and sent it do Washington," said the ASAC from Tennessee.

"OK. I'm in, but I want you to keep Senior Special Agent Zinck in the loop, as his people are working their asses off to keep on top of those Sheriffs and that mob of National Guardsmen running the recovery search. I'll work the SBI people and the AG in Raleigh, and keep you up on anything from that end. But when the time comes to make a big arrest or to pen an indictment, I want in on it. I have some favors to pay off in Raleigh, and it is an election year after all."

"Sure, Ashton. You can have any of that crap, when the time comes. So we're all agreed? Then let's get on with it," said SAC Dunbar.

"So what do we call this operation?" asked ASAC Williams.

"I was thinking, Operation Nanny, for the river's nickname," said SAC Dunbar.

"Sounds good to me," said Ashton. Williams nodded in agreement.

Two hours later, SAC Dunbar had arrived back in Atlanta, by helicopter, and was on his way down from the rooftop landing pad to brief his core staff.

He had already sent orders via Blackberry for his staff of thirty Special Agents and an administrative support staff to spin up the fusion centre for OPERATION NANNY. The fusion centre concept was necessary because it allowed liaison officers from other law enforcement agencies, such as the Swain County

Sheriff, the Department of Defense, the North Carolina Highway Patrol and SBI, and other agencies to be rolled together with his core FBI personnel. It made for a steep learning curve for the new players, who were not used to such a highly net-centric command post style of operations. But the close cooperation and trust that quickly develops from working in such close proximity often paid off hugely, because it really allowed the investigation to move at a much faster pace than when each agency is left operating in the dark, without the benefit of all possible information that could be relevant.

SAC Dunbar sat down at the command desk in the fusion center and opened up his secure laptop to review the data he had taken with him from the Asheville office.

His eyes scanned the files, which were organized according to time-tested FBI-standard Information Management protocols. It did not take him long to find the report he wanted to read, from Senior Special Agent Zinck:

"OPERATION NANNY. Post Interview notes re: Subject Captain H. Carter. After four hours, 36 minutes of standard POID interview, the session was terminated as no longer productive. Subject is agitated and aggressive but generally consistent in his story. He is intelligent and articulate. He appears sincere in the

desire for his daughter to be found. He is excessively curious about police of jurisdiction and investigatory details/procedures. He has been elusive about his activities in Tennessee. RECOMMENDED TASK: TENNESSEE FBI to determine when Captain Carter was last in Tennessee and follow-up with SAC Atlanta if there was a lie. RECOMMENDED TASK: ATLANTA FBI consider 24/7 coverage of Captain H. Carter in addition to the other POIs as listed in this morning's summary. RECOMMENDED TASK:CHARLOTTE FBI have NC SBI and all NC County Sheriffs shut down the air search as of Saturday AM, and draw down the volunteer ground / NC NG GSAR searches to no more than one search team of 20 or less, under Swain County Sheriff. RECOMMENDED TASK: have ATLANTA FBI contact Wing Commander at Dobson AFB to redeploy all military resources out of the search area and provide After Action Report to SAC ATLANTA FBI via DoD Liaison Officer. TAKE FOR TASKING: ASHEVILLE FBI will transition to care and feeding of this investigation after providing daily SITREP to SAC ATLANTA FBI by COB today. All further TASKINGS and RECOMMENDATIONS regarding OPERATION NANNY shall come from ATLANTA FBI or as directed internally from SAC CHARLOTTE.FBI. Signed Zinck, K.A. SSA."

"So Zinck thinks Ashton is going to try to hang on to this a little, eh?" SAC Dunbar said to himself out loud. "He's in for a shock." SAC Dunbar was about to type up a shit-gram to Washington about the lapse in judgment by Senior Special Agent Zinck for having revealed the first name of one of the other suspects – a minor breach in security – and for having omitted the error from his report – a much more serious error, but then thought better of it. He could use that against Ashton if he needed to, so he decided to keep that bit of intelligence under wraps for the time being.

SAC Dunbar had another five minutes before the scheduled start of his staff briefing, so he ran through the data in his mind, organizing his thoughts in preparation for ramping up his fusion centre team.

With the father of the Carter girl effectively a low-order probability, at least for the murder and the other abduction, that left the two other unknown suspects gleaned from Major Tyler's report, along with the 24 registered sexual offenders in the tri-state area who had not yet been accounted for, the 27 Nantahala region locals who came up excessively elusive during interviews, and the 45 tourists who warranted further evaluation. There were also 640 hours of video taken from gas station and bank machine cameras, and the seemingly endless flow of new tips being posted on the FBI and police websites.

He estimated the data would keep his fusion centre staff busy for months before the field was narrowed sufficiently to really wrap his hands around. Time to get down to some serious data mining and generally boring police work, he thought to himself with resignation.

The worst thing, he mused, was that less than 10% of child sexual predators are ever caught. And unless it turns out to be one of the known pedophiles or registered sex offenders, it could be anybody. It could be someone in a position of great trust and respect in the community, from Sheriff right down to the forestry staff or even military personnel −Lord knows there's enough of them who have become screwed up with substance abuse and post-traumatic stress disorders from serving in the recent wars in Iraq and Syria.

It could just as well be local citizens, itinerant recreation industry workers along the Gorge, or even someone from out of the area for that matter.

With the magnitude of the task before him now clearly visualized in his mind, he began dissecting it into task groupings which could be delegated to the various Senior Special Agents acting as Team Leaders and

Department Heads. As the elegant complexity of the investigation began to take shape in his mind the images of the two missing girls and the dead Gorton girl began to recede from his mind, as though they were ghosts.

The next morning, as SAC Dunbar sat at his workstation in the Fusion Center at the Atlanta FBI building taking in the morning briefing from the ASAC, Hank Carter was just pulling out of the campsite with the trailer attached to his minivan.

Nick and Marjorie had helped him pack up their gear but the three had spoken little to each other. They all felt that by leaving they were reducing Abby's chances for survival.

In one small gesture of hope, Nick went back to the stump that Abby and he had been using to chop firewood on the morning they had prepared breakfast for their parents, and slid a Ziploc sealed bag under the edge of the stump so that part of the letter was visible.

He had written the letter during the night, promising to be nicer to Abby and that he would stand up for her more at school. He ended the letter by telling her how much he loved and missed her.

For his part, on the drive home, Hank was thinking about what he would say to his Commanding Officer, but then gave up on that line of thinking. Obviously, Hank reasoned, he would get all the leave he needed to take care of his family and to try to hold himself together. But then what? What could he do from home to find out what is going on? Would the FBI keep him informed? What could he do?

The thoughts running through his mind became useless and repetitive, and kept returning to the question: *Who is this David?* And then it hit him, *David must be the primary suspect, and the FBI can't find him!*

For the rest of the drive home, Hank thought about where he would get the money to pay for a private investigator and what he would say to the man to get him to find out who this David was. He would also ask him to find out about any other suspects that the FBI and other police agencies were looking for.

He would conduct his own investigation and find his daughter, even if he had been told in no uncertain terms to stay away from the search area. He could work from his home in Atlanta, and not just sit on his hands.

The emotional and optimistic high lasted for several days. Just long enough to find and contact a private investigator.

Hank wanted to make an appointment with a PI that he remembered had done a job for his old Flight Commander when he went through his divorce. From what Hank remembered, the guy, Robert or Bob Stokes, had done some of the work for cash. That suited Hank very well, as he thought that he was about to do some things that he would rather keep off the books.

But this Mr. Stokes proved hard to find. Hank had tried calling his number several times, and had no way to be sure that his messages were even being listened to. The voice from the answering machine on the number he had gotten from the now retired major said nothing about being a private investigator, only to "leave your name and number, and what your problem is, and I will call you back. BS."

That "BS" comment could mean Bob Stokes, or it could mean that the voice belonged to a jerk. But just having left a message with a PI had given Hank and Marjorie some hope, even if only that someone might eventually call them. But within a few days there had been no call, and their initial burst of hope soon largely faded.

With each passing hour of waiting for the phone to ring, of searching endlessly through the Internet for stories about the 'Nantahala search', going through blogsites about the missing girls and fielding literally thousands of emails, tweets and Facebook posts, the Carters were becoming eaten up by their concern for with their missing daughter.

They felt guilty for any sleep they stole from their monitoring and searching efforts. They ate only sporadically and, increasingly, could not communicate with each other.

Long unspoken issues from years past would suddenly come up and become ammunition for the occasional blow-up of argument and blame, or worse, self-recrimination.

And as much as the parents spiraled into the hellish anguish, poor Nicky became withdrawn and silent.

Had his parents even thought about it, they might have realized that Nick was having suicidal thoughts. He was all alone in a very dark place in his mind, and could think of no way out.

They had tried to get him to resume his school routine and athletic activities, but that had fallen apart when Nick began assaulting any kid who had ever been cruel to Abby.

So all three of the remaining Carters were confined to their home, stewing in the foul juices of their grief.

10

B. S.

Hank and Marjorie were arguing in the kitchen again. But rather than walk away as he had so many times before, for some reason Hank wanted to stand his ground. It could have been because he was waiting for the coffee to brew, or that he had been about to make himself a sandwich, but for some reason, Hank stayed in the kitchen and just let Marjorie continue raining her accusations down on him.

"If you had taken that job with American Airlines, like Bruce and Jenna did, then none of this would have happened!"

"First of all, Bruce took the job. Jenna went along for the free ride. She hasn't worked a day since they got married, and you know it."

"Well, she was a pilot, wasn't she! And she looks after their home, just like I do. But that's not the point. You and your Air Force bullshit. You just want to be in uniform, and you don't care about what it does to me and the kids. And now look at us! Abby is GONE, Hank. She's GONE, probably DEAD, and it's all your fault!"

Hank sighed, not wanting to even reply to that.

"And what have you done about it? You can't even find a Private Investigator in this entire city! You are useless!"

"Have you had enough, Marjorie? Or do you want to dump more shit on me?"

"You're the one who knows all about this shit!"

"Is that the best you can do? Come on, Marj, you can do better. Give me your best shot!"

"OK, Mr. Perfect. How about this. Maybe she just ran away! Did you ever think about that? Huh?"

That was a new one. In their weeks of grieving over Abby, Marjorie had had more than a few blow-ups, and accused Hank of everything from being responsible for her death to having failed to chase after the van when he had first seen it. But the idea that Abby had run away was a new one.

"If she did run away, it would have been from you, Marj, not me."

Hank regretted his words before he even saw Marjorie's reaction.

She was speechless, shocked and deeply offended at what Hank said. It hurt her, deeply, because she felt that it could be true. She had rejected Abby at birth, calling her 'someone else's baby'. Hank would never forget it when he first presented Marjorie with the slippery, newborn, placing her on Marjorie's chest. She stared at the baby as if there had been a big mix-up. "This is not my baby," was the first thing Marjorie had said.

In contrast to the loving way Marjorie had reached out to accept Nicky when he was born, she seemed to shy away from the newborn Abby, and seemed to hold her newborn as if she couldn't wait for a nurse to take the infant away.

Hank knew at the time that it was just some type of post-partum depression. Marjorie had been a wonderful mother ever since. But her bond with Abby never really achieved the depth of love and closeness that she had with Nicky, and Hank knew that it bothered her.

He had made up for this disconnect by giving Abby extra attention himself. But it had always been a sensitive topic for Marjorie, who carried the shame of knowing she had rejected her baby, and could not get over it or forgive herself.

Her only way to handle it was to hit back, yet again.

"I'm not so sure there ever was a white van! I think you made that up, to cover your tracks," she accused.

Hank shook his head, realizing that their fight had reached a level of absurdity that he could not stand for any longer. He turned to leave the kitchen, and was just walking away when the phone rang.

Hank nearly jumped out of his skin, and Marjorie was shocked into silence.

They both stared at the phone. It had not made a sound for days.

Picking up the phone, Hank answered: "Carter Family."

"Hello, this is BS. You left a message on my machine. You worked with Major Anderson?"

"Yes. I wanted to consult with you on something."

"Don't say anything more. I'll come over, and we'll talk in my car. Is that OK for you?"

"How soon can you be over here? I'm at —"

"I know your address. What good would I be to you if I couldn't even figure that out. I am right outside, come out now." Click.

Twenty minutes later, Marjorie rushed to Hank when he came back into the house. He brushed right past her, and went to his filing cabinet to retrieve two gold coins from his EOTWAWKI stash. From his days of reading a variety of End-of-the-World-as-we-Know-it genre novels. He had become a gold bug. All that had come of it was an excessive supply of canned goods, a frightened wife and kids, and a small stash of gold and silver coins.

When the end of the world did not come, and Hank had moved on to other things, the silver and gold had remained, taped to the back of each of the four drawers of his filing cabinet.

That he rushed back out to the waiting Bob Stokes, with a couple of gold coins in hand, told Marjorie that Hank had made a deal with the private investigator.

Not wanting to be left out when Hank came back, Marjorie set out a plate of cookies and two cups of coffee and sat at the table, hoping Hank would talk to her. She felt terrible for what she had said to him, and wished she could take it all back.

An hour later, Hank returned. When he saw Marjorie sitting there in her best 'forgive me' presentation, he was pleased. It had long been their way of making up after a blow-up, to sit together at the dining room table and have some sweets, and talk about anything but what they had just fought over.

"I like him," said Hank.

"You hired him?"

"Yes."

"To find Abby?"

"No. He said he would not take that job, that it was too big for just one investigator. What he agreed to do was to investigate the investigation, to find out what the FBI and the various Sheriff departments in Georgia, North Carolina and Tennessee are doing."

"What good is that?"

"Marj, nobody is telling us anything. If we only knew more about what's going on in the investigation, we could handle this better. But that's not all."

"What else?"

"I asked him to find out who this 'David' was, that Agent Zinck told me about in Asheville. And to run down some of those suspects we read about in the paper, up in Tennessee."

Hank smiled inwardly at the humor he and Bob Stokes had shared, when Hank explained how much it pissed him off, not knowing who David was. Bob had said, "So now the name, 'Dave' is a four-letter word to you, eh?" to which Hank had enthusiastically agreed. It was nice, Hank had thought, to be sharing a laugh with another guy. He decided that the high cost of hiring the private investigator was worth its weight in gold, quite literally.

"So he's going to find out who this 'David' suspect is? Why are you so obsessed with this David guy, anyhow?"

"Marj, we've gone over this a dozen times. I think he's the guy with the van I saw. I have to know if they found him, how he is, and if he has anything to do with Abby."

"I know, I know," Said Marj, agreeing that it could be positive, embracing the plan. "You done good, Henry Carter. But how much did it cost to hire him. You gave him gold?"

"Yeah. He wanted three grand, so I gave him two of those Canadian Maple Leafs. He said it would take him up to two weeks, but that he would give me whatever he got as it came in. So he's paid in full, and now all we have to do is wait. He'll contact us, and then I'll meet with him."

"Meet him? Where?"

11

LIFE WITHOUT SUNSHINE

Like two ships passing in opposite directions, distant but aware of each other, Hank and Marjorie seemed to be going through their tragedy as two isolated people – not drawing any strength or support from each other, not giving each other any help.

It seemed to both of them that life had lost meaning. Other than to keep constant vigilance for that knock at the door, telephone call, or email that would break through the gloom, they had no hope.

Marjorie had taken to working on scrapbooks and photo albums of all things Abby, as though it would somehow keep her from disappearing out of her life.

For his part, Hank took his cue from Marjorie and began sorting through the variety of digital pictures and videos that the Carter family had accumulated over the years since they began having children. He did not focus solely on Abby, as he was aware of how badly Nick was doing. Having something to do, in re-formatting, organizing, archiving, and in some cases editing the video material helped to pass the long hours.

One evening, Marjorie and Hank spent a rare few hours together watching the videos from Abby's first two years.

"Oh, I remember that! That's when Nicky first started his Engineer phase," said Marjorie as they watched Nicky, 5 years old at the time, loading Abby the space monkey into the cardboard rocket ship that he had designed.

Hearing his name, Nick quietly joined his mom and dad at the couch and watched videos that he had never seen. But after a few minutes enjoying seeing himself with his baby sister, he began to cry. He couldn't take it for long, watching baby Abby laughing and playing with him in the video.

Marjorie listened to the sounds of his sniffles as Nick withdrew to his bedroom in the basement. She thought about going down to him, but decided to let him have a good cry first.

Another video had started, this time with just Hank and Abby, in the master bedroom. Abby had her head on Hank's chest, but was wide awake.

"Sa-sha!" she demanded.

In the video, Hank complied, singing the Sunshine song to her. Hank watched himself singing the lullaby to his baby girl. Soon enough, Abby was asleep on his chest and the video kept running for another minute, with Abby's mess of curly blond hair rising and falling with each breath that her father took. Hank realized that his baby girl truly was the sunshine of his life.

Silently, Hank and Marjorie sat together on the couch, with tears streaming from their eyes. There was nothing to say. They simply sat there feeling miserable in their life without sunshine.

The scrapbooking and video editing projects had been abandoned now for weeks. It was as though all three members of the Carter family had decided to turn away from anything that reminded them of their pain.

Nick was the only one who had been able to find something new to occupy himself. He had begun a floor-to-ceiling purge of his formerly very cluttered bedroom. It was not clear even to him what his motivation was, but Nick started to take everything that had ever been special to him and breaking it down into the smallest possible pieces, and then packing the residue into large orange garbage bags he had found in the Garage.

All of his sports trophies and posters of his favorite athletes had been removed. His extensive collection of Star Wars action figures – some of which were original collectibles from the 1970s, still in their packaging - were now in tatters and bagged along with the other refuse of his former joys.

His CDs and video games, along with three generations of Sony gaming consoles had been disassembled and broken down into unrecognizable bits of thermoplastic and circuit boards. Even his collection of snow-globes, treasures from a time when he believed in Santa Clause and the magic of Christmas, were now broken bits of glass and porcelain.

When he was done his room was as tidy and antiseptic as a bathroom at a doctor's office, and just about as warm. Had Hank or Marjorie even noticed they might have been concerned that Nicky may have been putting his affairs in order in advance of suicide. But they did not notice.

However it was not Nicky who was in truly dire straits. The excision of the trinkets of his childhood had been, for Nick, his own version of survivor's grief therapy. He was working through the necessity of moving on from the pain he felt at having lost his only sibling by reinventing his identity, transforming himself into a solitary and emotionless young adult, someone who had no need for toys or sentimental things. Things that brought painful memories, and guilt.

The newfound maturity with which Nick was, without any guidance or help, attempting to chart a healing course was demonstrated by his attempts to intervene in the downward spiral of his parents.

One evening, Nick had come upstairs to see one of his parents sitting at the dining room table, drinking Scotch.

Nick had experimented with alcohol with other boys from Pace Academy and a few times alone down in his bedroom, but he did not like the way his head felt afterwards. He hated the headaches and the spins, and soon rejected alcohol completely.

But to see one of his parents obviously drinking far too much, with a variety of empty bottles in disarray in what had once been a well-stocked liquor cabinet, it was obvious to Nick that something had to be done.

He approached quietly and took a seat at the table, and moved close, gently intruding.

"Mom, you can't do this," he said, simply.

She embraced Nick, too destroyed by grief and exhaustion to say a word. Her tear ducts had been depleted from hours of crying. She was in very real pain, both physical and emotional. Her heart was full of anguish and her head was full of banging hammers, pots and pans.

She held Nick, thinking of Abby, and squeezed him so tightly that Nick had difficulty breathing. But he did not try to break loose. He had to be there for his mother, so he endured the painful hug as though it would take some pain away from her. And it did.

After holding each other for perhaps fifteen minutes in silence, they separated.

Nick looked at his mother's face. She looked awful. She looked like someone had poured some vile black liquid onto her face and pepper-sprayed her eyes, they were so painfully red. The creases etched in her brow and in the now permanent frown on her face made her look like an evil old woman, not the joyous and loving mother she had always been.

And then she spewed projectile vomit all over his face.

The disgusting heat and stench shocked Nick into action. He wiped his face with his hand, and then lifted his mother from her chair and guided her gently upstairs to her bedroom.

Once there, he took her into the bathroom and stood her up in the shower, fully dressed, in the master bathroom.

After making sure the water was not too hot, he turned the shower head on and held his mother under the spray with his strong arms.

Barely aware of what her son was doing to her, Marjorie closed her eyes and relaxed, with the warm water cascading over her face and head.

Her moment of relaxation ended abruptly when another surge of nausea came up. She doubled over and threw up onto the floor of the shower.

Somehow this made her become a little more aware of her surroundings. She rose back up to a vertical posture and began clawing at her clothes.

Nick was uncomfortable with the chore, but he helped his mom remove her sweater. When she seemed to be capable of continuing on her own, he spoke to her.

"Mom, you need to get out of all those clothes and get in bed. I'll find you something to wear and put it on the bed, ok?"

"Yes, Henry."

"Mom, it's Nicky."

"Nicky. When did you get so tall?" she muttered. But she was making progress with getting out of her clothes, so Nick left her alone and went to the bedroom.

After finding some panties and a T-shirt and placing them on the bed, Nick walked out of the master bedroom and went into his father's study, just down the hall.

As he waited for the computer to come to life, he heard the reassuring sounds of Marj crashing about in the bathroom and then climbing into bed with a moan.

"OOOH, my head hurts! Nicky! Get me some water!"

"OK, Mom, but don't drink too much water, you'll just throw it up again."

"That's fine! That might get some of this *poison* out of me. OOOOH, that hurts!" she moaned again, with her hand on her forehead.

When Nick put a glass of water on her bedside table, he was pleased to see that his mom had put on a T-shirt and was comfortably settled in bed. She was soon fast asleep.

Eleven hours later, at about eight am, she woke up and made her way to the kitchen, in her bathrobe.

Hearing this, Nick came up from his bedroom, where he had been busy moving his furniture away from the walls in preparation for repainting his room. His plan was to use the tin of white paint he had found in the garage to make his room seem brighter than the deep blue colors currently on the walls.

"You're alive! Mom, it's great to see you awake!"

"I don't feel alive. How did I get to bed? The last thing I remember was sitting in the dining room. Wait a minute, did I throw up on you? Or was it a bad dream?"

"It was both, Mom! You puked all over me!"

"Oooh, I'm sorry, chipmunk," she said, turning to look towards the dining room. It was cleaner than it had been in months. Nick had taken care of the mess.

"You cleaned it up?"

"Yes, Mom. It was pretty stinky."

"And what happened to the bottles?" she asked, noticing that the liquor cabinet was completely empty.

"There is no alcohol in the house anymore, Mom," he said, simply.

Marjorie stood there for a minute, thinking about the implications. Her child had taken control, making an adult decision and acting as though she were the child.

She was so proud of her son, and so ashamed of herself.

"Thank you, Nicholas Erin Carter. You did good."

"You're welcome, Mom. Now, let's try to get a little food into you. We have a big day today."

"What are we going to do?"

"We have to go shopping. I need new clothes and you need to get out."

"Oh, not today, Nicky. I feel like crap."

"No, Mom. Today. We need to get you out of here, out into the sunshine.

12

PRESCRIPTION

Hank picked up the phone on the second ring. He did not hear the nearly inaudible double click as the Digital Collections System automatically activated, recording the conversation into the DCS-1000 databank at the FBI Atlanta Division under a date-time-group file tagged OPERATION NANNY – CARTER RESIDENCE. Simultaneously, the DCS-1000 generated a text-to-transcript document that enabled a powerful computer to search the conversation for a variety of key words. The automated system also sent a text message to the shared OPERATION NANNY account, where it popped up as a single line 'chat' entry on the half-dozen secure computers of the crew on watch at that time in the fusion centre.

The same 'chatter' was also pushed out to the Blackberries of two Special Agents, sitting in their sedan down the street from the Carter residence. Recognizing the warbling ringtone, Special Agent Dunwoody picked up his blackberry and thumbed the icon for the 'listen in' application, and held the unit up to his ear. With his other hand, he jotted down the time of the intercept in his notepad.

"What's happening?" asked Probationary Special Agent Yeoman, sitting next to Dunwoody.

"We got an intercept. Shhh, I'm listening."

Eighty yards away, in the Carter residence, Hank had answered the phone.

"Hello, Captain Carter speaking." Hank had taken to answering the phone with his Air Force rank despite the fact that he had been grounded from flight status and placed on indefinite medical leave.

Major Snow, the Wing Flight Surgeon, had consulted with the counseling psychiatrist that the FBI had referred him to, in support of the case management of Captain Carter's medical file. The call from Pastor Sullivan had given him a hint at what to expect.

The Commander of 94th Airlift Wing had not decided if the intrusion of law enforcement types would be beneficial to the well-being of one of his personnel. While there were no clear directions in the orders that fit the current situation, Colonel Taschuck had permitted the contact between Dr. Kevin Peel and the Wing Flight Surgeon, on the advice of a fellow colonel with the Judge Advocate General, and the advice the Wing Surgeon had received through the medical chain of command. But it did not make Colonel Taschuck feel any better about the situation. The Air Force usually took care of their own people in their own way, but given the seriousness of the situation whic one of his pilots now faced, the Wing Commander thought it best to keep Captain Carter at a bit of a distance from work, and give those concerned the time needed to find a resolution to the difficult circumstances.

When consulted by Dr. Snow about having Carter work in some sort of office job, such as Wing Operations, Dr. Peel had recommended sending Hank home on stress leave, and that he should ultimately be placed under the medical, and if warranted, psychiatric supervision of Dr. Peel.

Major Snow had thought it odd that Captain Carter had not yet seen Dr. Peel, but agreed to comply with his advice. Dr. Peel explained that he preferred it when patients sought him out, whether through the mental health support team at Dobson, or in a more casual referral through a pastor or other person of trust. As Peel explained, he had a number of pathways which Carter could find him through, and thereby continue to feel in control of his own life. This was essential to Dr. Peel's therapeutic approach, and held the best prospects for a good outcome and the eventual return to duty for Captain Carter.

Of course, there was more to it. By creating the conditions whereby Captain Carter would voluntarily reach out, Dr. Peel felt that there would be less resistance to his unique combination of psychotherapy and pharmacological treatment. In order to place Hank Carter in the right frame of mind for the deep psychotherapy, he would also need to be on a progressive cocktail of rather strong psychoactive drugs.

Sitting in his Peachford Road office after hearing Dr. Snow's confirmation that he would have access to Captain Carter's medical records, with a view towards treatment, Kevin Peel turned his mind to the actual course of treatment.

Peel thought it through. First, he would start the patient off with a low dose, perhaps 100 milligrams daily of carbamazepine USP, commonly known as Tammitol. Once the patient had settled into the more pliant frame of mind that this sedative would cause, he would then add in the more powerful, 200 milligram daily dosage of the hallucinogenic drug psilocybin, to open the door to the patient's darkest fantasies. Once the patient had adapted to the routine of drug – enhanced psychotherapy, with the fantasy role-playing and articulation that he would gradually build up through the twice weekly therapy sessions, he would then add the third element of the cocktail, the stimulant CX717, that would bring the fantasies to the status of virtual reality. Only then, thought Dr. Peel, could he liberate the patient's mind, having brought him to an altogether unimaginable level of cognitive power, where dark fantasies from the collective unconscious would become glorious works of art in an auto-cognitive realm of lucid dreaming. At least, that was the goal. The process of taking an anxious, troubled but otherwise sane man to this state would require taking him right to the edge of insanity, and then beyond.

Of course, he would not have been able to experiment so radically on patients without the support of the Defense Advanced Research Projects Agency, that provided him both his supply of highly stressed military patients and the permission granted by Department of Defense and Defense Advanced Research Projects Agency, DARPA, for the use of CX717 in a non-monitored level IV drug trial on the military patients, at Dr. Peel's sole discretion. This arrangement with DARPA gave Kevin Peel carte blanche over his patients. This power was wielded by a researcher in psychotherapy with little regard for the patient. Only the results mattered. His ego drove him to publish or perish. The Peel Personality Inventory Test was only the beginning of his need for recognition by his 'peers'.

Eager to begin working on the unsuspecting Captain, Dr. Peel thought about his favorite poem:

> *I wander through each chartered street,*
> *Near where the chartered Thames does flow,*
> *And mark in every face I meet,*
> *Marks of weakness, marks of woe.*
>
> *In every cry of every Man,*
> *In every Infant's cry of fear,*
> *In every voice; in every ban,*
> *The mind-forged manacles I hear:*
>
> *How the chimney-sweepers cry*

Every blackening church appalls,
And the hapless soldiers sigh
Runs in blood down palace walls.

As he reflected on what he could remember of William Blake's poem, *London*, Dr. Peel thought about how important his work was. To him, it was the realization of Blake's own view that it was our fundamental lack of imagination that imposes concepts of good and evil, and that it was in the projection of artificial human mores onto the natural world that our puny thoughts act as shackles on the natural human spirit. Reality is a construction of limitations that we place upon ourselves – the 'mind-forged manacles'.

The treatment itself came with risks, especially at the start. The Tammitol made the patient more susceptible to ideation fantasies, which was part of the treatment, but it also came with a considerable suicide risk. But that was a risk that Dr. Peel was willing to take. Once the psilocybin kicked in, the patient would be far into altered sensory perceptions and transformed self-body images. The contextual cues of the ideation and fantasy constructs that Dr. Peel would evolve through the psychotherapy, would make Carter far too engaged in the alternative reality to ever consider suicide. He would then feel a god-like and totally uninhibited euphoria.

At least that was his theory. In practice, Dr. Peel's 'disinhibition therapy' was still an unpublished, rather questionable experiment. But based on the success he was having with the PTSD clients that DoD had referred to him so far, he felt that he was on the verge of rocking the foundations of his profession. When he thought about it more, Kevin Peel imagined himself modestly accepting his Nobel Prize.

Perhaps it was in response to no longer putting on his uniform, or simply a familiar piece of his old life that he missed, but Hank needed to feel strong. He was barely holding together. Perhaps he was just one more outburst away from being heavily sedated and locked up in the psychiatric ward.

What really got under Hank's skin, which he had no effective way to deal with, was the constant looks and comments of sympathy. As one gives another who has lost. But to Hank, these innocent gestures were infuriating, in part due to his helplessness – the inability to take any effective action – and in part because it made him feel like everybody believed that Abby was dead. She is not dead was the feeling it evoked, along with impotent rage.

What Hank dearly needed was something to give him some hope. In his depressed state, he had completely forgotten about his conversation with the private investigator he had hired the week before.

He picked up the phone, unaware that he was not the only person listening.

"Hank, it's Bob Stokes. I got something."

"What is it?

"Don't say it, you never know who's listening."

"OK. Go on."

"You remember that four-letter word we talked about?"

"Yes. You find…it?" asked Hank, having just stopped short of saying 'him'.

"I did. But I have not done a full work up. I'm going into that other place we discussed, so it's too far out of my way. You want the other info, it'll cost you a couple of days, so another grand. Have the money with you next time we meet, if you want the extra service. Otherwise I'll just give you the other stuff you have me doing. Clear?"

"Clear. So now what? How do I get the info about the four letter word?"

"It's in your mailbox. Go get it now. Good night, and you are welcome." Click.

In their cruiser, Agent Dunwoody looked at his junior partner, who had been listening in with a second ear-piece rigged to the iPod.

"Did you see any deliveries tonight?"

"No, there was just some kids going door to door, asking for sponsorship for their hockey team. I got their names and phone numbers when they went around the block. They checked out. Besides, when they went to the Carter home, nobody came to the door," said Yeoman.

As he thought about the implications of what he missed, and wondered at what Carter meant by 'four letter word', Special Agent Dunwoody sat powerless as he watched Captain Carter open his front door, look around the neighborhood for a moment, and then take a small white envelope out of his mailbox. Hank looked at it and saw there was no stamp, just "HC" in large letters where the address would normally go. He quickly went back inside and closed the door.

Hank took the envelope to the dining room table, opened it and read the single page.

The Dave character the FBI is interested in is David Seiprecht. He lives at 127 Wildwood Road, Rainbow Springs, Macon County, NC. He is a registered sex offender on the national and the NC lists, and had been in prison on murder charges until the week before your daughter went missing. He got off on a technicality, and was released directly from the courtroom in Franklin, NC, on May 10th. I'm on my way into Tennessee now on those leads you wanted me to run down up in Knoxville. BS.

Hank smiled at Bob's initials. It was the first time he had genuinely smiled in weeks, and now he had something to live for. Something called hope.

From what Bob Stokes had said, he could wait till next week and pay Bob to go up to Franklin to research David Seiprecht, or he could go up there himself.

With a newfound sense of purpose, Hank decided he would go to Franklin himself and see what he could find.

He would have to find a way to do it without tipping his hand to whoever was sitting in that government looking car that seemed to be watching his house.

Perhaps he was being paranoid, but Hank was starting to think of himself as an outlaw, someone who had to sneak around. This was annoying, but somehow invigorating at the same time.

He had a mission.

13

FRANKLIN

Hank had been keeping to himself, but was not oblivious to the change in behavior of both his son and his wife. But whenever they had tried to include him in their activities, he had closed the door on them, walked away from them, or simply put a pillow over his head and ignored them.

So they gave him a wide berth and did what they could to bring more light into the home.

Fresh flowers were on the tables here and there, and home-cooked meals were actually served at 'normal' times.

But Hank was not ready to rejoin the living.

That was the way it had been until he received the message from Stokes. Now, after weeks of being mired in depression, suicidal thoughts and literally days without leaving his home, Hank Carter had some inspiration. He would go after David Seiprecht himself. While Stokes worked on the investigation at large, he would uncover Seiprecht's secrets and then move in on him and rescue his daughter. A solo covert mission.

For a moment, Hank considered that with Abby having been missing for over six weeks that his daughter was most likely dead. It was not the first time that he tormented himself with the thought. And if that were true, then the only thing left for him would be retribution. But on the chance that Abby was still alive, and finding Seiprecht would take him to her, there was no point being pathetic and hanging around the house.

Hank gave his head a shake. No, he was not ready to accept the notion that Abby was already dead. He did not feel that in his heart. He still felt a glimmer of warmth and joy buried deep under all the pain and anguish, the recriminations and doubt that he and Marjorie, and even Nick, had been going through.

And he knew where to start. He needed *data*.

With blood on his cheek from a hurried job of shaving the six or seven days of growth from his face, Hank grabbed his leather jacket, wallet and keys, and headed out the door. The newfound sense of purpose and cool morning air began clearing the depressive fog from his mind.

If any of his Air Force colleagues from Dobson AFB had seen him, dressed casually in blue jeans and hiking boots, they would have been surprised at the transformation. Hank looked more like a logger than a pilot, and had a new look of determination in his eye.

He didn't even go upstairs to the couple's bedroom to inform Marjorie about his new plan. There was no point. Other than momentary bits of calm, like last night, the chasm between Marjorie and Hank had reached epic proportions. She was an emotional wreck, going from high to low on a daily basis, the highs out shopping in the daytime with Nicky, and the lows around the house with Hank in the evenings. Hank didn't want to risk trusting her to keep his plan a secret. She would understand that his disappearance would have something to do with the name they learned the night before. That would have to be enough for now.

As he backed the minivan out of the driveway and pulled out onto Woodlands Drive, he was aware of the black sedan of the FBI agent tasked with the morning

Carter watch. Rather than the annoyance and hostility he had felt in the past, the presence of the agent tailing him no longer held any negativity for Hank. The guy was just doing his job. So rather than trying to lose him he simply accepted the unnecessary presence. Who knows, he thought, it could come in handy to have them around at some point.

Less than two hours later, Hank pulled into one of the 45-degree parking stalls on Main Street West in Franklin, North Carolina. Hank sat in the car for a few minutes going over the map from his AAA book, to refresh the layout of the town. The map was well detailed, indicating the locations he intended to visit. He thought through the sequence and then folded the map and put it back in his pocket. Then he gave some thought to the agent who had followed him to Franklin, and smiled to himself at how hard he was about to make the poor guy work for his next paycheck.

His first stop was the Angel Medical Center. After walking around in the public areas for a few minutes to give the agent enough time to decide to enter the building, he approached the nursing station slowly, as if he might have already had a conversation, and then made an overt show of noticing the agent. Hank then hurried out of the hospital, forcing his FBI shadow to decide whether to investigate what had transpired at the nursing station, or rush to stay on task.

Hearing the footfalls behind him, Hank was certain that the agent was stuck to him like glue. Perfect.

Hank then made similarly short and inexplicable visits to the records office in the bowels of First Presbyterian Church, the Student's Union office at Southwestern Community College, the small local newspaper office in Palmer Street Shopping Center, and the Franklin Gem and Mineral Museum. Then, just for the fun of it, he spent over half an hour wasting the time of a loans officer at United Community Bank.

The constant walking around the small town felt good to Hank and it was made that much more enjoyable as he thought about the effect he must be having on the poor field agent.

After having a quick lunch at the Blue Ridge Roadhouse, Hank hoofed it across the bridge to the east side of town, to pop in to the Macon County Sheriff's office to capture as much information as he could from the Sexual Offender Registry. Hank had already checked both the North Carolina and National lists over the internet, but he wanted to see if there were any local resources such as posters or leaflets that could give him some additional clues.

By the time the agent followed him inside, Hank had already picked the place over and gleaned whatever he could. Nothing new was found. He had taken a quick high resolution digital image of the "wall of fame" that posted the photographs of all the officers of the Macon County Sheriff's Office. In most of the pictures they were dressed in their crisp white uniforms. However in some of them, the men wore their dark browns.

Being proud of his military service despite the hiatus that the Base Flight Surgeon had put him on by withholding his flight medical status and ordering stress leave, Hank still felt a profound respect and fellowship for other men and women in uniform in any manner of public service.

After taking a moment to read the organizational chart, look at each and every deputy's photograph and read their names and ranks, Hank was ready to move on to the next stop in his Franklin itinerary. But when he looked around and saw he was alone, he decided to take down the poster and quickly folded it and stowed it in a large pocket of his jacket. Hank thought to himself, 'it never hurts to have a hard copy'.

He was just a few paces from the door when a man suddenly approached him.

"Hello there, friend. I don't think we've met before. I'm Deputy Martin. What's your name?" said a friendly young man.

Hank took him in with a head to foot inventory. He noticed that the man's shoes were perfectly polished. They were not the patent leather shoes with the permanently baked-on shine that so many Air Force officers had taken to wearing. This young officer's shoes were spit-shone and hand-polished, almost like those of a new recruit.

Going by the razor-sharp crease in the man's grey pants, the blazing white uniform shirt, the pristine white gloves tucked neatly into the man's thick black patrolman's belt, and the golden strand of rope hung on the man's left shoulder, Hank surmised correctly that the man was on some form of parade or other ceremonial type of duty.

"Pleased to meet you, Deputy Martin. Quite a nice detachment you have here. Have you been serving here long?"

"Three years, Mr.?"

"Wow, just three years? So how did you pull the ceremonial detail?" Hank asked, gesturing at the man's gloves.

"You're sharp, what are you, in the Service?

"Yup. I'm over at Dobson, in Atlanta."

"Really? So a pilot or something?"

"Something like that. Hey, it was nice to meet you, Deputy. See you around!" Hank said.

"And you are welcome to keep the souvenir you made out of our org-chart!" said the bewildered man to Hank's back.

That should keep the FBI agent busy for a few minutes, thought Hank as he passed through one door while Probationary Special Agent Yeoman was coming in the other, looking flustered and confused. It was his first field assignment without his supervisor, Special Agent Dunwoody, and he did not want to screw it up by losing his assignment.

Hank got lucky and hailed a 'Larry's Taxi' right in front of the Macon County Sheriff's Office.

"Where to?"

"Just let me out by the War Memorial on Philips, at Main Street, thanks."

"Aww, come on, man, that's not even worth picking you up for," said the driver, not completely joking. "Wouldn't you rather take a scenic tour around town?"

"Well, if you want to have some fun and make some coin, I'll give you a hundred bucks cash right now if you'll dump me off at the memorial – that's it there, on the left, isn't it?"

"Yeah. And?"

"And then you rush back to where you picked me up and let the FBI agent tailing me hail you. Take him right out of town. Tell him I switched cabs and was on my way to the airport or something."

Smiling as much at the chance to make a fast buck as to screw with a G-man, the driver immediately caught on. "You got it, bud!"

Hank tossed him the cash and jumped out of the cab. He pretended to be headed to the crosswalk while he kept the corner of his eye on the taxi. After the cab squealed around the corner and raced down towards Palmer Street for the one-way return to the bridge across to the Sheriff's Station on Lakeside Drive, Hank reversed course and strode quickly past the short line of trees in front of the Macon County Courthouse, and went inside.

Hank figured that he had at least fifteen minutes before the FBI agent would figure out the ruse. It took precious minutes to find the appropriate wicket, ask the clerk a couple of questions, and pay the twenty dollars for the thick document he had requested.

By the time Yeoman finally found him, Hank had made it all the way back to his minivan parked almost a block from the courthouse and had tossed the documents inside.

Hank lazed around on Main Street eating an ice-cream purchased at a convenience store near where he had parked. After giving the agent a few minutes to see that he was in no hurry to go anywhere, as if he had just decided to drive from Atlanta to spend the day exploring Franklin, Hank was ready to go home. He had what he came for.

Hank walked the few yards from the sidewalk bench he had been sitting at while he ate his cone and conducted his amateur version of counter-surveillance. He was suddenly surprised to hear a voice addressing him by name.

"Excuse me, Sir, aren't you Henry Carter?"

"Yes, I am. What can I do you for?" Hank said, now curiously surprised.

"Well, my name is Kevin Peel. I'm an associate of your military pastor, Sullivan."

"How did you find me?" asked Hank, incredulously.

"Find you? Not at all, I'm in town on business."

Growing uneasy at first, Hank shook the small man's hand. "You've got me at a loss. How do you know my name?"

"Well, let me start by offering you my condolences on your loss," he said.

"Loss? What the fuck are you talking about, Mr. Peel?"

"Your daughter."

"My daughter? Who the hell are you?"

"I'm sorry. Please let me begin again. I am a psychiatrist and a grief counselor, and –"

"You're that quack!" Hank interrupted, furious. "The one Pastor Sullivan's been trying to get me to call? The one who's been calling my wife?" shouted Hank.

"If by 'that quack' you mean to say, am I the one who has been attempting to help you and your family with your grief, yes, I am." Peel said this defensively, growing fearful that this encounter would not go the way he had hoped. He needed his experimental subject, and had immediately gone to Franklin when he heard of the FBI pursuit, as his authority as the governmental psychiatrist kept him in the loop.

Things had gone much smoother with Marjorie Carter, when Kevin Peel had intentionally run into her at her local Walmart. She had immediately taken to him, and had been talking with him for over a month. She had agreed with Dr. Peel that she should keep her therapy from her husband, until he had come to terms with his own grief and was ready for help, as Dr. Peel had succinctly put it.

She had seemed eager to be prescribed anti-depressants, which made life easier for Peel. A medicated patient is a stable patient, after all.

In his interviews with Marjorie, he had quickly determined that she had a bag full of issues for him to dig into. Not only were there deep seated insecurities which seemed to be complicated by unresolved post-partum depression, but she also seemed to be nearly paranoid about not being included in whatever Hank did concerning Abby. It was as if she were co-dependent, and yet her husband, from all accounts, was not. Peel found her to be pliant and cooperative, but also found her to be disappointingly unimaginative. She was of little use to his work on disinhibition therapy.

The one area he found intriguing was her receptivity to suggestions that there were incipient sexual overtones to the relationship between her husband and their daughter. Of course, to develop this line of thinking in his patient, he would ultimately need access to all members of the Carter family, which had proven to be difficult.

But now, with Hank Carter standing right before him, and not responding to his presence in the cooperative manner that he had hoped for, Kevin Peel could feel hairs on the back of his neck rising, adrenalin flowing and his heartbeat galloping away from him. He recognized this as the fight or flight response, and felt like a trapped animal about to be attacked. He thought about running away from the big, angry man that had, until now, been his prey.

Close to throttling the man then and there, Hank reminded himself of his newfound mission in life and realized that he had to change tactics immediately or lose an opportunity by scaring the creepy little psychiatrist away.

"I am sorry, Dr. Peel, is it?" Hank began again, trying to look sincere and apologetic. He actually lowered his shoulders and hunched his back in an attempt to look the wretched, grieving father that everybody expected him to be. Hank sighed, calming himself before he went on. "I guess I can't put it off forever."

The psychiatrist seemed to grow two inches taller as Hank's tone changed from aggressive military man to the sort of pathetic, lost, wreck of a person that he liked to work with.

"Put what off, Henry?" he cooed reassuringly, as if he already had Hank on his interview couch.

"Talking. Talking to a shrink like you."

"Go on, I'm listening."

"Pastor Sullivan told me about you, when we were up the Nanny on the search for Abby. But it was just too tough back then to talk to anybody. Marj and I... We." He stammered convincingly.

The distraught look on Hank's face became genuine, as he thought about the first days home in Marietta without Abby, when he and Marj had spent so many sleepless nights waiting for the phone to ring, wringing their hands impotently and staring at each other with the self-recrimination and blame that they had quickly fallen victim to.

"I understand. Those first weeks must have been horrible for you all."

"They were." Hank had him, and decided to reel him in. "Look, I don't want to do this here. Can we do this some other time and place?,

"Sure. Here's my card. Just call my secretary, Bessie 'the cow', when you want to come in," said Kevin Peel, suppressing his excitement at finally getting through to his latest test subject.

Hank was startled by the cow comment, and thought Dr. Peel to be a little bizarre, but pressed on with the charade.

"I'll come by one morning. I see from your card that your office isn't far from Pace. I'll come over after I drop Nicky off at school."

"Pace? Yes, I have a few other patients with kids in Pace. It's a great school," said Peel, trying to keep the conversation going a bit longer. Finally having access to the Carter family was fulfilling an urgent personal need.

Hank was certain that there was something strange or false about this Dr. Peel, but also found him easy enough to handle. Time to break it off and leave the quack wondering, Hank decided.

"That's enough for now, Doc. I'm going home. By the way, what are you doing up here in Franklin?"

"Er, I'm just following up on some work I do for the courts, over at the penitentiary, with the inmates and remands." He replied without thinking first, and immediately regretted having given out so much information.

"How interesting. OK, Doc, see you soon," said Hank as he quickly got into his car, and Dr. Peel watched him drive way.

Both men felt that they had controlled the other.

Probationary Special Agent Yeoman had taken a couple of photographs of Hank and the unknown man, and recorded the time and place in his field notepad. As he got into his car and drove off to pick up the tail, he felt that he had accomplished a great deal despite having nearly lost the subject a couple of times. He quickly forgot about the gap in coverage when he had been taken for a ride by a cab driver. The agent never knew what he had missed while Hank had been in the Courthouse.

14

RESTRAINT

This time Probationary Special Agent Yeoman was in the driver's seat, when the iPhone app informed him that there was a call going through at the Carter residence. He activated the transmission mode, put the phone to his ear, and jabbed the dozing Special Agent Dunwoody in the ribs.

"Call coming through to the Carters," he said.

"Give me that," ordered Dunwoody, taking the iPhone from Yeoman, checking that the simultaneous transcription was flowing across the small screen as he listened in.

"Hank, it's Bob Stokes. I got something. Meet me at the usual café."

"What have you got? Tell me now," Hank demanded.

"No. I think it's better we meet and discuss this in person. You'll understand when you hear it. Ten minutes." Click.

With no choice in the matter now that Stokes had hung up on him, Hank headed out to his minivan and drove to meet the private detective.

As soon as he entered, he noticed Carol looking at him in the sympathetic, caring way she had since she first tried to console Hank over the disappearance of his daughter.

"Oooh, Hank," she said, as she hugged him closely.

When Hank tried to pull away from her unusually tight embrace, she held on that much more tightly, whispering into his ear. "Your friend Bob says the Feds have this place under surveillance and your phone is bugged. He wants you to meet him in the library over at Southern Polytechnic. Take my car, it's parked out back," she said, excited to be involved in an adventure. She slipped her keys into Hanks back pocket. Not completely by accident, she felt his buttocks in the process. "Go now!"

Hank felt her hand in his back pocket, sensing the keys being deposited, but was oblivious about Carol's hand having lingered there longer than necessary. Without missing a beat, Hank walked past her towards the bathroom and slipped out the back door.

Special Agent Dunwoody assumed that Hank was washing his hands before the meeting. He had surveilled Carter in this very café before and it had gone smoothly each time. Stokes usually arrived a few minutes after Carter, looked around nervously, and then joined him in one of the booths along the side of the café, where the windows overlooked the parking lot. This time it was different. Hank seemed to be taking too long in the bathroom, and Bob had still not shown up. By the time Dunwoody got suspicious and went to the washroom to check, Hank had already pulled Carol's VW Golf into the parking lot nearest to the library at Southern Polytechnic, not far from the hangar line at Dobson AFB.

Hank found Bob Stokes sitting in one of two armchairs set at ninety degrees to each other in a quiet corner of the library.

"OK, Stokes, I'm here. And thanks for setting things up with Carol. Why is the FBI still watching me so closely?"

"They're probably just trying to keep a continuous record of your activities. It's standard practice for a suspect in a major crime."

"So I am still formally a suspect? I thought all of that was behind me."

"No, it never ends until they arrest someone, and even then it can continue if they just don't like you. But you're not alone, they've got a number of other suspects. They always keep the parents on the short list because more often than not it's a family affair." When Bob saw the anger rising in Hank, he softened his tone. "Relax, I know you didn't do it."

"How do you know?"

"I found him."

"Who, the guy with the van?"

"Yes. But you're not going to like this."

"Why?"

"The guy with the van is indeed David Seiprecht, the guy you gave me to run down."

The blood ran out of Hank's face. He knew all about Seiprecht, from the transcripts he had obtained in Franklin the week before. Hank had thought about the possibility that Abby had come to great harm, but he had held out hope that it would turn out to be kidnapping for ransom, or for prostitution, or something else. But not the evil things that a real monster like Seiprecht was capable of.

"Tell me. All of it."

"There's not that much to tell. You may even remember, about six months ago. Remember that fireman, Gary Freeman, who was found beaten to death up in Macon County?"

"Bob, I've read the transcripts. So tell me something I don't know. You found his van?"

"You mean the van he borrowed," corrected Stokes.

"You know what I mean."

"It's important to be precise," said Stokes, "But yes, I found the van that the FBI are still looking for. Here's some pictures," he said, thumbing through digital images with his smart phone.

Hank immediately recognized the van from the windows covered with tin foil to the strange bend in the bumper. The photo looked recent.

"This is the van I saw that day. What are those panels?"

"That's a sea container. The vehicle is hidden in one of those sea containers, in a little quarry behind the Nantahala Recreation Centre – back behind that Relia's restaurant. I don't think the van's been on the road for over a month. The tire tracks are all washed away, and the last rainfall was about a week after Abby went missing."

"How did you find it?"

"Well, I cross checked the list of registered sex offenders with the license and registration databases in all three states. I had to call in a lot of markers, by the way, and that came at a cost. You'll have to add another two grand to my fees for this week. Anyhow, I got a hit, and it was the only hit in our region. So I drove to his house and sat on it. Then he was dropped off by a Deputy from Macon County Sheriff's Department. Turns out they have hauled him a few times for questioning, along with all the other guys on the registry. Some of my LEO buddies say they interviewed him for 48 hours straight, before releasing him, and he's climbing their list of suspects. The FBI are still in charge, they call their investigation "OPERATION NANNY", relating to all three girls – that dead Gorton girl, the girl from the gas station, and your daughter."

"So why would the Macon County Sheriff's Department interview him, and not the FBI?"

"Oh, it's a huge task, so the FBI uses local LEO's – local law enforcement - to vet the list of POIs – Persons of Interest, because the Sheriff's departments keep pretty good tabs on all the local creeps in their counties, and they do a great job running them down and putting them under pressure.

Anything that comes up promising, they send over to the FBI officer in charge, the Special Agent-in-Charge, guy by the name of Dunbar. He's the guy in charge of everything, and the guy who has hacked your computer, your phone, and has agents on you 24/7."

"I want to know more about how the FBI works."

"Sure. Later. Anyhow, as soon as this Seiprecht guy was free, he got right into a smaller car – registered to his mother and he drove right up to the Nantahala."

"So where did he go?"

"He drove up to the quarry and just drove slowly past the sea container, as if he was checking that the lock was sealed. Then he went right back to Rainbow Springs, where he lives."

"Where's that?"

"It's like fifteen miles west of Franklin, on Highway 64"

"So did you break into the sea container?"

"No, not right away, I had to follow him home first. Then I went back to check what kind of lock it was. It was an easy one to open, a typical Master padlock with a five-pin tumbler, so it was easy to trick it open," said Bob, casually. Hank listened intently, for Bob to continue.

"And there it was, driven nose-in. And he had been in a hurry when he parked it - the side mirrors were both broken off on the way in. See here, in this picture?" Bob showed Hank a digital picture on his iPhone. "So that's good news."

"Why is that good news?"

"Because the vehicle is not 'clean'."

"You mean, it will have evidence in it?"

"Yeah. So I didn't touch it. I just took these pictures and made sure that there was nothing inside it, no bodies. Sorry. Nothing obvious. You can see in these pics. Sorry about how dark it is, the darkened windows blocked out most of the flash, but I took this one on night mode. You can see that the van is empty. Just a few rags on the floor."

Tabbing through the pictures, looking for anything that could help in his quest, Hank eventually gave the iPhone back. "Yeah, empty. And the rest of the container was empty?"

"Yeah, completely empty. I made sure to check that, too."

"So what's my next move?"

"Well, we could do an anonymous tip to the FBI and let them process the vehicle. That's my advice to you. It would break their investigation wide open."

"Yeah, but I'm not sure. Something feels wrong about all of this. I mean, why has it been so hard for them to find this guy. You did it in what, five days?"

"Yeah, but I'm good. They would have gotten there eventually," Bob paused, seeing the skeptical look on

Hank's face. "What? Don't you think the FBI wants to get this guy?"

"Sure, but I think there's more here than meets the eye."

"Well, it's your dime, and your daughter. I've done my job. If you want to be paranoid, and I'm not saying you don't have good reason, but it's your daughter's life, man. Don't be a jerk. Call the feds and tell them everything. I'll cooperate with them completely, no charge," he said, somewhat angrily.

"OK. How do we do it? Just drive there?"

"Well, we could just phone them, but there would be a bit of a lag while they go up and down their chain of command. I think there's a better way, that would guarantee results."

"What's that?" inquired Hank.

Ten minutes later, Bob Stokes and Hank arrived back at Rosalind's Cafe. Hank gave Carol her car keys and a big hug, which Carol leaned into warmly. Then Hank walked out the front door, towards his car.

He pretended not to notice the two late-model sedans parked on either side of his minivan, nor the surprised looks on the faces of the three Special Agents hanging around, not far from his car.

He got into his car and accelerated out of the driveway.

As the three Special Agents jumped into their two cars to follow Hank they eventually noticed that Bob Stokes was now following them, bringing up the rear of the formation of four vehicles. Bob was capturing video of the slow-speed pursuit with his iPhone with one hand as he drove with the other.

By the time Hank had led the agents over the state line into North Carolina, Bob Stokes had sent Agent Dunbar the images of the white van, making sure that the Georgia plate of the van was visible.

Within minutes, a technician in the fusion centre had tracked down the registration of the vehicle and reported to Special Agent-in-Charge Dunbar that the vehicle was registered to a man with a clean record, who worked at the same abattoir that David Seiprecht worked at, just west of Asheville, NC.

He then sent the same images to a specially prepared address list of television media personalities who had been featured prominently in the news during the short-lived media frenzy of the initial search of the Nantahala area. Thumbing with his right hand as he drove, he added the phrase: '*Missing van located near NOC. FBI about to arrest suspect in Rainbow Springs, in Macon County, NC.* He hit 'send'.

Even driving just ten miles per hour over the speed limit, Hank was impressed to have collected a flock of police cars in his wake. It seemed surreal to Hank. None of them had their sirens on as they still did not have the full picture. Word had gotten out over the police nets that something was about to go down in the Nantahala, but they still did not know the exact location, so they simply followed Hank.

As he drove past the exit for Highway 64 westbound, just before Franklin, NC, and continued on towards Highway 28 to the Nantahala Gorge, Hank was relieved to see one of the FBI vehicles take the off-ramp and head west on Highway 64, towards Rainbow Springs, presumably to arrest David Seiprecht.

Half an hour later, Hank pulled his vehicle up to the sea container in the quarry. FBI vehicles along with cruisers and SUVs from Macon and Swain County Sheriff's departments pulled up and parked all around.

No less than three helicopters took up positions a few hundred feet above the quarry.

Right on cue, Bob Stokes pulled up and parked close to Hank's minivan. Bob walked right up to the sea container. Bending over to trick the lock, it took less than a minute to open the door.

With a great deal of satisfaction and feeling hope for the first time in a long time, Hank approached the container, coming to a stop just behind Bob Stokes.

After rotating the locking lever arm and swinging it into the detent on the right hand door, Bob pulled the left hand door open.

Hank's heart sank to the dirt. He could not breathe.

The container was empty.

For a long few seconds, the throng of Sheriff's personnel and FBI agents stood around waiting for something to happen, or stared into the empty container. Those who looked at Hank Carter saw the look of surprise and anguish on Hank's face. Some of them, particularly those with children, felt empathy for Hank.

Their shared moment of disappointment was suddenly broken by some shouts from the Swain County

Sheriff, standing in the open door of his cruiser, with his radio hand-set in his hand. "He's on the run! Get moving, boys! He's five miles up Silvermine Road, booking it! Deputy Craddock, you and Jake take your cars up Silvermine. Watch for the reporter's helicopter overhead, they're right on top of the van, calling it in on Channel 16." The two Swain County deputies sprung into action, sending gravel flying into other vehicles parked nearby in the quarry.

"Deputy Fraser, you take your Macon County guys back up highway 28, and go around to the south and then head west on Tellico Road. Call ahead and get Sheriff Singer to send some cars over to block up Wayah road near the county line."

"That's 'Detective Sergeant Fraser, Sheriff', said Sergeant Fraser, moving slowly to his cruiser as if to prove a point.

"What the fuck is the matter with you, Sergeant. MOVE!"
shouted Sheriff Clarkson, losing his composure for a moment.

As the Macon and Swain County Sheriff's men sped away, it took the State Troopers who has just arrived at the quarry a bit longer to figure out what was going on, and they asked Theo Clarkson.

"What frequency are you guys on? Aren't you monitoring Channel 16?"

"Well, we normally do, Sheriff, but we were using our Ops frequency to get orders from Raleigh. What did we miss?"

"Well, It appears that Mr. Carter here and his private investigator, that's him there, Mr. Stokes, may have found that white van we've all been looking for. They led us all here in some kind of parade to the post, only to find this sea container empty. But it looks like Stokes here had sent some info to the media, and one of the airborne reporters saw the subject van leaving the quarry just before we all got here. That was about ten minutes ago. The helicopter's been following the van up Silvermine Road at the speed of heat, and now we've got our boys chasing from this side, and Macon County Sheriff's personnel closing off the south side."

"Got it, thanks, Sheriff. Anything we can do?"

"Well, trooper, I guess you could cordon off the area around this sea container and sit on it until I tell you who is taking it over. That'll free up some of my resources."

"Sure thing Sheriff. Anything we can do to help you out."

With just the two troopers and Sheriff Clarkson the only others left in the quarry, busy talking together near their cruisers, Hank and Bob were left standing alone close to the sea container. The area had gone from chaos to silence in the span of just a few minutes.

Emotionally exhausted at the highs and lows of it, Hank was resigned to wait to find out what would come of the air and ground chase.

Following Bob's lead, Hank walked into the container. The two men walked the entire length and found nothing. Just empty space.

On the way back out, Hank saw a small black object on the floor, and picked it up. It was a piece of hard rubber. He showed it to Bob, who knew what it was right away.

"That's a piece of a boot, broken off the sole. Looks like a Vibram sole, like you are wearing, Hank."

Hank lifted his boot backwards, to look at the distinctive sole pattern on his right boot, and compared it to the walnut sized chunk of rubber in his hand.

"It's evidence, Hank. Leave it for the feds. And let's get out of here. We've already contaminated this scene with our own footprints," Bob said, leading Hank out of the steel box.

But Hank did not put the piece of boot-sole back down right away. He held on to it tightly, as if it could somehow speak to him, tell him where his Abby had been taken to. It was the first solid piece of hope he had, something he could hold on to, something that gave him hope. But Bob was right, he had to give it to the feds. Maybe their CSI team could make something of it.

Hank reluctantly gave it to one of the Sheriff's deputies who had come in to shoo he and Bob out of the crime scene.

Twenty minutes later, the Feds had seized the van from the Macon County Sheriff's Department who had found it. The full force of the FBI was brought to bear on the evidence, with a swarm of agents appearing out of nowhere to process the sealift container back at the quarry. The van itself had been winched up onto a flat-bed truck, and driven out from where it had been found, where Silvermine Road had overtopped the ridge, and become a rutted and dried up 4WD track leading down to Fairview lane into Macon County.

Special Agents from the FBI office in Asheville had worked with the Swain and Macon county Sheriff's personnel to conduct a manhunt, but even with a dog team up from Franklin, they had not been able to pick up the trail. It had gone completely cold by the time Detective Sergeant Fraser had found the van and reported in over the radio.

Sheriff Clarkson had handed Hank and Bob over to Special Agent Zinck, who personally drove them to Asheville to be interviewed by some Special Agents heading up from Atlanta.

The FBI spent eight hours interrogating Hank, and just two hours on Bob Stokes, whom they were satisfied had simply been doing his job as a private investigator. The agents from Atlanta had already read the transcripts of the conversations between Hank and Bob, along with the surveillance reports from Special Agent Dunwoody and others who had witnessed Hank and Bob, at Rosalind's Café, in Marietta. They were confident that Bob had cooperated fully, and not held out on them.

But he had, on just one detail.

When they released Bob, the FBI agents thanked him, and told him that they appreciated his efforts to convince Hank to lead the FBI to the sea container, and let the professionals handle the discovered evidence. They encouraged Bob to stay out of the investigation from this point on. Bob assured them that he was done with Hank Carter and accepted his keys from Yeoman, who had been given the task of retrieving Bob's car from the quarry.

But they really gave Hank a good going over. Despite the new evidence, and Hank's full cooperation. Senior Special Agent Zinck still considered Hank to be a suspect in his own daughter's disappearance. Hank started to hate the guy, even though he believed he was being treated fairly by the other agents, interrogation being what it is.

While the crime lab agents were busy measuring, taking photographs, pouring plaster casts of footprints and vehicle tracks at both the sea container and the area where the van had been abandoned, Senior Special Agent Zinck made Hank go over his witness statement yet a third time. He seemed to be making a show of it, always standing to one side, as though he were making sure he was showing his front side to an audience.

Hank realized that it was just like in the movies. There were people standing on the opposite side of the mirror, watching the interview and perhaps deciding his fate.

On the other side of the window were a couple of Zinck's subordinates, someone from the NC State's AG office, and two other guests.

They could all tell that Hank had been consistent, but that he was also getting very annoyed at the treatment. He was crashing, on the verge of a nervous breakdown. The only thing he was holding onto was the hope that they were giving David Seiprecht an equivalent treatment.

"I think that's enough. Cut him loose," said a voice in the viewing room opposite the interview room.

When Hank was escorted out of FBI office in Asheville, and told that he was free to go, he was bewildered that they were not even doing him the courtesy of driving him back to his car. Nobody had said anything about his vehicle, or how he would get home. They just walked him to the door and held it open for him, and closed it behind him after he passed through.

He just stood there, on the concrete steps in front of the building, almost catatonic. He did not even register the man walking directly toward him, nor the Swain County Sheriff's Department emblem on the door of his car. Sheriff Clarkson had come by to collect Hank and take him out for a drink. Theo Clarkson knew that someone had to tell Hank, so he had arranged with

Probationary Special Agent Yeoman that Swain County would take care of getting Mr. Carter back to his car.

Sheriff Clarkson took Hank by the elbow and led him towards his cruiser. Hank, lost and confused after the day's events, complied without commenting.

"Henry. Can I call you Hank?" asked Theo Clarkson, as he drove north on highway 28, back to the Nantahala Gorge.

"Hank's fine, Sheriff."

"Listen. I'm sorry we couldn't have had much of a conversation back in Relia's during the search. But I want you to know, I know what you are going through."

Hank did not respond, so the Sheriff continued.

"I've got an 11-year old daughter and two older sons myself, and Sandy and I take our kids camping all the time. And I know that you are not involved in any of this shit."

Hank turned his head slightly, listening.

"Anyhow, Hank, I know you've been treated roughly by that asshole Agent Zinck. He's done that to literally dozens of witnesses during this investigation. It's his job, you know, to be the asshole that puts people into a corner to see what they will do."

"He certainly does that," agreed Hank, starting to warm up to the Sheriff. It was the first time any of the enforcement types actually talked to Hank, man to man, and not treated him like an annoyance, or worse, a suspect.

"What did they tell you, about the investigation?" asked Sheriff Clarkson.

"Nothing. They basically just said 'thanks for the help. We'll take it from here."

"Not surprising. We generally don't like civilians getting involved in investigating on their own."

"I'm not a civilian, Sheriff."

"Yeah, I know, you're with the Air Force. That's why a lot of my guys feel for you, because you are in uniform. But there's a few out there, in other agencies and in high places, who like you for the crime, you know?"

"Yeah, I know. I've got a few names, and I'm starting to 'know my enemy'. I just can't figure out why they keep coming back to me."

"It's because they don't like unsolved crimes. The SBI guys from Raleigh are generally more interested in getting a conviction than they area about solving the crime. But some of their newer CSI technicians are much better, more interested in following the evidence."

"Are they working on the van?"

"No. That was passed on to the FBI."

"Will you find out what they learn? Pass it on to me somehow?"

"Sorry, Hank, I can't do that. Besides, I'll be one of the last to hear. No, your best bet is to lay back in Atlanta, and let the feds do their work. It takes time, in situations like this, with no real suspects."

"What do you mean, no real suspects?" Hank asked.

"This is what I was afraid of. Nobody told you?"

"Told me what?" Hank was getting upset, with a wild-eyed look a man has just before he goes berserk.

"They let Seiprecht go. The van was not his, and the guy who had lent it to Seiprecht now says that it was reported stolen over a month ago, before the girls went missing."

"You have to be kidding me! I am sure that it was Seiprecht I saw in that van, I've seen his photo! I could recognize that creepy little goatee anywhere!" Hank sounded desperate. "Aren't they even going to process the van, find some DNA evidence or something?"

"I'm sure they will. There were enough other witnesses who saw a van that matched the description, but there is nothing so far that links him to it during the timeframe we are concerned about. And there's more, something I have been instructed to tell you."

With his heart sinking, knowing that his one hope for an end to his ordeal had gone up in smoke, Hank prepared for yet another body blow.

"What."

Sheriff Clarkson took out a document from his breast pocket.

"This is a court order from the Superior Court, in Asheville. You are under a restraining order, to stay out of the State of North Carolina and to stay at least 500 yards away from Mr. David Seiprecht, or you will be arrested.

Shocked, Hank just stared at the Sheriff for a few seconds. "You have to be shitting me!"

"No. This is real. He lawyered up as soon as Sergeant Fraser escorted him home. His lawyer was in the courthouse within two hours, claiming that you are obsessed with him, harassing him, and that your grief over your missing daughter makes you a danger to him, an innocent citizen wrongly accused, yada yada yada."

"Un fucking believable! Come on, Sheriff, you know this guy's involved, somehow, don't you?"

"Hey, that's not up to me. All I can tell you is that he lives in Macon County, not my sandbox, but I will have my boys keep an eye on him if he enters Swain County. That's the best I can do."

As they arrived at the quarry, and drove up to Hank's minivan, Hank barely registered the FBI Agents taking plaster casts of the footprints surrounding the sea container.

As he got out of the Sheriff's car, and opened the door to his minivan, he turned to the Sheriff, trying to think of something to say. He understood that this would be the last time he would be in Swain County.

As Sheriff Clarkson looked into Hank's face, he watched Hank look up and down the gorge, and then stare at the river, clearly thinking of his missing daughter.

"Sheriff. Thank you for talking with me. I don't blame you for this shit. And you're my only hope here. Please don't give up on Abby. She *is* alive, I feel it in my bones. And if anybody can survive, whatever happened to her, it's Abby. She's an amazing little girl, and we can't give up on her. She won't."

Hank was in tears as he got into the vehicle, and started the engine. Looking straight ahead, out the front window, he did not see how Theo Clarkson was struggling to hold back his own tears, thinking of the missing girls.

"I'll follow you back to the State Lines, where Agent Dunwoody is going to take over and follow you home. They're going to sit on top of you from here on out, Hank, so my advice is to do nothing out of the ordinary, don't come back to North Carolina, and don't get into it any more with your Private Investigator."

"OK, Sheriff, I'll stay out of it. But you let me know whatever you can, if there is a break. Nothing is going to stop me from coming back here when you find Abby. Nothing." Hank said, with finality, before driving off. Sheriff Clarkson followed at a respectful distance.

After they reached the state line, and Theo saw Dunwoody pull in behind Carter's minivan, he turned back into Macon County, heading to visit Sheriff Albie Singer. Something was bothering Theo Clarkson.

As he pulled his Swain County cruiser into the line of Macon County cars and got out, he noticed that Sheriff Singer's car was not there. *No matter*, thought Clarkson, *what I really want to do was examine the evidence log.*

In the back of his mind, for some reason he recalled the moment he had tasked one of Singer's men, Sergeant Fraser, to go back and secure the scene at the gas station. A few days later, when Clarkson followed up with the gas station owner, he said that he had given the disks from their security cameras to one of the Macon

County men. But the only evidence that had been referred to in the daily situation report out of Macon County during the first week of the search phase had been disks from the interior security cameras. Yet Sheriff Clarkson had confirmed that there was also an exterior camera observing the area, from the pumps all the way over to the propane tanks.

Probably the disks are all there after all, thought Sheriff Clarkson, *but I may as well check with the evidence clerk, to make sure the FBI in Atlanta have been given all the evidence.*

15

COUCH

Finding Dr. Peel's office had been difficult. The street address was 2157 Peachford Road, yet the numbers jumped from 2153 to 2161, with apparently no Number 2157.

After driving around the block several times, Hank parked the minivan. He got out and walked up and down the block. After he passed 2157 he noticed that there was a gap between the architect's office he was passing and the next brick building, a small rental property office, Medlock & Son's Realty.

No more than a yard wide, the corridor between the two buildings was freshly paved with interlocking paving stones. The brickwork appeared to have been refurbished recently.

Exploring, Hank walked the ten yards through the space and discovered a large courtyard with drive-in access from the laneway beyond, to the rear.

There was a solid wooden staircase leading up to exterior decking on the second floor, so he went up. At the top, he noticed that there was a shiny brass "2157" on the door immediately to his right.

At first annoyed that Dr. Peel would have such a difficult office to find, Hank forgot all about it right after he entered the Doctor's office. The girl who greeted him was that much of a distraction.

"Hi, you must be Henry Carter?" said the pretty young woman. In her late twenties, she was wearing a black and white patterned summer dress, that, when taken with her big brown eyes and voluptuous figure made Hank imagine her to be the most attractive 'cow' he had ever seen.

He chided himself for even thinking of her in those terms, only to confirm his earlier intuition when he looked around her workspace. Everything in her domain seemed to have the same black-and-white cow motif. Her coffee cup had a cow on it, her pen-holder was crafted out of small white fence-planks with a plastic cow in a coral, and there were all sorts of magnets, picture frames and other paraphernalia all relating to cows.

"I can't believe what I am looking at!" Hank said, laughing.

"Yeah, awesome, aren't they," she said, simply.

Then hank remembered what Dr. Peel had said up in Franklin. "You are such a cow, aren't you?" Hank said, unable to resist.

"You got it! The name's Bessie! And I love everything about cows, as you can see! Hey Doc, your patient is here!" Bessie shouted in the general direction of the open door farther back in the office.

As Hank looked in that direction he had the distinct impression that Bessie was raised on a farm and was proud of it. She was a psychology grad-student working on an inter-disciplinary thesis under Dr. Peel's supervision. An assistant as uninhibited and friendly as 'Bessie the Cow' could only aid Dr. Peel in his approach to his younger patients. Children would flock to her like flies.

"Henry, come on in," said Dr. Peel, appearing in the doorway to his office.

As Hank walked into the psychiatrist's office, he looked around the room. There were a few unusual pieces of art on the shelves at the back of the room, and a small collection of Bonsai trees on a lighted, stand-alone shelf. Then he noticed a few framed photographs on one wall and walked over to get a better look. Two men in desert-patterned army fatigues stood side by side, brandishing knives that must have been nearly a foot long. To Hank Carter, these did not look like standard military pattern knives, or even bayonets, but more like something a survivalist might treasure.

"That was Iraq," said Dr. Peel.

"You were in the military?"

"Not exactly. I do some work with the Department of Defense, military clients dealing with anything from anxiety and depression to full blown PTSD. Those are patients of mine."

"Oh? They live around here, in Atlanta?"

"No, not exactly." Changing the topic, the doctor gestured to a comfortable armchair near a corner of his desk. "Make yourself comfortable."

"Thanks." Hank sat down and watched Dr. Peel make his way around the desk to sit in his chair of authority. Hank thought to himself, *this is one arrogant man.*

After some trivial and polite conversation, Dr. Peel switched tracks and guided the conversation in a particular direction.

"How has your wife, Marjorie, been holding up?"

"Not so well. She has been in a very dark place, as have I, to be honest. We went through several weeks of anger and frustration, and then started fighting. She blamed me for not keeping an eye on Abby, and she blamed herself for not being closer to her."

"You said 'had'. What's changed?"

"Well, it's strange. After we really bottomed out a couple of weeks back, when we watched some videos of Abby and Nicky, something happened. She had been drinking a lot, and got so drunk one night that she threw up all over Nick. From what she told me, that was the turning point. Nick cleaned her up and took care of her, and then got her to go back out into the world by asking her to take him shopping, of all things. Somehow Nick was the first one to start to turn things around and pull himself out of his own funk."

"And Nick is Abby's older brother, right? How bad were things for Nick?"

"He's five years older than Abby, he's now fifteen. Both he and Abby had birthdays in the last few weeks. Abby is 10 now." Hank paused, with a far-away look in his eyes. "We celebrated Abby's birthday without her this time."

After another short silence, Hank got back on track. "I sort of lost track of what Nick's headspace was, but he was really down. He kept getting angry with kids at school, lashing out for no reason. Then he stated his 'list'."

"List?"

"Yeah. He had made a list of the kids who used to tease and bully Abby, and posted the list on the internet as a 'hit list'. By the time he had worked his way down to about number five, Pace Academy caught on and called the police."

"What was he doing, killing them?" said Dr. Peel in a tone that was strangely intrigued, as if he was not completely joking.

"Just about. He beat the crap out of one of them. He was lucky not to get a juvenile assault charge.,

"Understandable. He must have been in a great deal of pain over his sibling's death."

"Death? What are you talking about!"

"I'm sorry, 'disappearance'. For Nick, after this length of time, the grieving process he is going through is much the same as for the confirmed death of a loved one."

After thinking about whether to punch the doctor out, or continue sitting still for this garbage, Hank regained his cool.

"Well, I think it's worse than if she were dead. I mean, at least then we would know. For me, the not knowing is what's driving me mad."

"And how have you been holding up?"

"I feel like a caged lion. I want to be out there, doing something to help find her, but the FBI and the cops are keeping me out of the picture."

"You want to be involved in the investigation?"

"Yes, or out there, searching. Doing nothing, just sitting around the house, is like being locked in prison."

"Have you had any suicidal thoughts?"

"No way. I've had murderous thoughts, like when I think about what I would do if I get my hands on whoever has my daughter."

"Go on," said Dr. Peel, with more interest than he showed.

"Well, I would just kill him, with my bare hands."

"Have you fantasized about killing? Like, how you would do it and how you would feel afterwards?"

"Fantasized? No, not exactly. I just get steamed when I think that she could be in the hands of a depraved person, and there's nothing I can do to help her. She's all alone. She's just a ten year old child."

"What was your relationship like with her?"

"Fine. We are very close."

"How close? Were you intimate with her?"

"What the fuck are you talking about?" Hank could not hold back. "Are you sick, or something?"

"Sorry, but it's something I do sometimes. To get a sense of your mental state. Your reaction tells me a lot about how well you are holding up."

"This does not sound right. Is this how other psychiatrists handle their patients? You are a real psychiatrist, aren't you?" Hank asked, angrily.

"Absolutely. Actually, my specialty is in dealing with deviants, like child abusers, psychopaths, sex offenders and others who have deep antisocial and deviant behaviors. Much of my work is for the prison system, evaluating inmates and preparing psychiatric assessments for the courts. So my approach is not always suitable for 'normal' people like you," Kevin Peel said, making the parenthetic signs with his fingers as he bookended the word 'normal' with clicks of his tongue..

Hank thought about the transcripts he had picked up in Franklin the other day, and what he had read of Dr.

Peel's testimony. He tried to keep his anger from showing. He needed more information.

"Well, it makes me uncomfortable when you talk to me like that. There's none of that crap going on in my family and I find it offensive that you even hint at that."

"Understandable."

"But now that you mention it, Doc, what sort of person can do that kind of thing, I mean be a predator like that? I mean, are they animals, or do they know what they are doing and just don't care?"

"Oh, you would be surprised. From their point of view, they are actually morally and philosophically superior to society at large."

Hank's face became knotted in incomprehension.

Dr. Peel tried to explain. "Yes, they are not bound by the mundane social pressures and mores that constrain the rest of us, and pursue their venal pleasures with the vigor and gusto of the pure predator – of the *lion*. They have no guilt, no fear, and they experience satisfaction and exhilaration at a level that you nor I will never have access to."

"You say that as though you admire them, Doc."

Dr. Peel paused, slightly smiling to himself before replacing it with a more serious expression on his face. "Not at all. I simply try to understand things from their

223

point of view, so that I can accurately gauge what form of therapy or treatment would be beneficial to their well-being."

"I thought that there was no cure for that sort of thing, like pedophiles and rapists, that they will always re-offend."

"Well, the form of therapy I provide for some of my patients is not aimed at rehabilitating or curing them, in part due to the recidivism you mention."

"So what does your therapy do for them?"

"Well, it helps shape their...appetites, into a more manageable form. In a sense, I can gain their trust and get inside their fantasies, and then make subtle suggestions as to which other directions they could take their fantasies, thus taming or even domesticating their baser instincts." The self-aggrandizing conceit that Hank sensed from the strange Dr. Peel was revolting. Hank was certain that the psychiatrist was becoming overly excited as he talked about the perverts.

After having endured as much of the quack as he could take, Hank's brain followed the instincts of a predator and moved in for the kill.

"It must give you a great deal of satisfaction to be able to understand and manage their fantasies like that. But what about perverts who are not your clients?"

"What do you mean?"

"I mean the ones who are not in prison. The ones who are still on the loose. Do you work with the cops to profile them, or to find them?"

"Oh yes. I consult with all levels of law enforcement. In fact, I have published a few books on the subject. My latest, 'The Art of the Profile', is being used widely in the field," he said with great pride as he took a copy of his book from the bookshelf behind him, and passed it to Hank. "Feel free to take it with you," said Kevin Peel.

"Really? Thanks! Tell me more," Hank said casually, examining the repugnant doctor's book. Captain Hank Carter then shut his mouth and listened.

16

NICE GRANNY

Sitting in the small trailer, Hank and Bob Stokes had once again fallen off the FBI's grid. Yeoman was not all that concerned, as the behavior of Hank Carter had become plain porridge lately. The subject had been following a routine of therapy sessions with that respected psychiatrist, Dr. Peel, and had been spending time working out at the military gym.

Were it not for the fact that a courier had attempted to deliver a package to the Carter home, and nobody had come to the door to receive it, recently promoted Special Agent Yeoman would not even have picked up on the fact that Hank had somehow left his home without the agent noticing.

Hank had simply walked through his back yard and down the alley, to be picked up by Bob Stokes.

Seated in the motor-home Stokes had picked Hank up in, now parked in an empty parking lot by a vacant industrial building, Hank opened up a large yellow envelope and pulled out a thick set of documents. Then he reached into his pocket and took out three gold coins, which he smacked down onto the table.

"First, the money. These are the last of my gold coins. If you need more money it will take time to gather without it being picked up by the Feds. But these three coins are worth, what, almost six grand?"

"Yeah. That'll cover my costs for a bit. After that, you'll have to come up with more money. This is a kind of danger pay. I've already been warned off working for you, you understand?"

"Yeah, yeah, but for this I am still expecting your full calendar, until the money runs out, right?"

"You've got it, Henry. So what's the assignment now? Still going after Seiprecht?"

"Yes, him and a few other creeps, but focus on Seiprecht. And I have something for you to work with. First, here are some transcripts from the trial and the appeal from his murder charges. You know, the Freeman murder he got off on? Well, I went through them and made some notes where I think there could be some leads. There's also a chart I prepared with timelines, when he has been in and out of prison, and some newspaper articles I've dug up on him. The other files are pretty thin, just to get you moving on the right guys on the FBI list."

"Henry, where did you get these names? I couldn't get that much on my own, even with my contacts."

"From the quack."

"The one from the Seiprecht trial? Dr. Apple or something like that?"

"Peel. Dr. Kevin Peel. The guy is a complete jerk. I have to sit through a couple hours of his bullshit every week, pretending to be soaking up his pearls of wisdom while spilling my guts to him, just to get him talking about the profiles of the suspects he has worked up for the FBI. He's a real sieve, you know. He'd never last a week working for the Air Force."

"You know, Hank, you would make a pretty good detective," Bob Stokes said with respect. "So what are we really looking for? You know where Seiprecht lives, and we know that the cops didn't find anything in that van. So what's the target here?"

"His family. His past friends. Past employers. Work-place associates, like the guy he borrowed that van from. I want you to figure out all of his potential resources. Vehicle types, plate numbers, residences. What are his 'special' places? Places he's been in the past, or has access to. But I don't want you to follow him, like the last time. You know what the cops said to us about that. Also, I think the guy is more dangerous than you think. I think he really did beat that Freeman guy to death, and I don't want that to happen to you."

"I get the picture. So you want to find out where he could be hiding your daughter?"

A pained expression came over Hank's face, as if he had been pulled from the vigorous man on a hunt to the grieving father, from a world of hope to one of utter despair. "Yeah. And I'm prepared for what you might find," Hank said grimly. "Also, can you find a way to look into his driving records?"

"I'm with you, to see if he has access to any other vehicles, other than the two we know about?"

"Yeah. And one more thing."

"What is it?"

"I need a gun."

"Why don't you –." The private investigator cut himself off, remembering that the police had confiscated Hank's 9mm after they found it in his car, fully loaded, no trigger-guard, and without a carry permit. Carter had led the police on a wild-goose chase to North Carolina with an illegal weapon. He was fortunate to have skated past the possible charges that could have been laid.

"I'm not sure I can do that for you. I have relationships I have to maintain with the law enforcement types. But what I can do is get you some useful things you can carry legally that could prove helpful if the need arises."

"Well, if that's the best you can do, I'll take whatever help you can give me."

"So let me ask you, what will you do if I find it?"

"Keep this to yourself."

"Of course."

"I'm going to find my daughter – alive."

"Let's hope so. But what about him?"

"Oh, he's dead. He's very fucking dead."

It only took a few days for Bob Stokes to find what Hank was looking for. Their meeting was so rushed this time around that Hank could not lose the agent babysitting him. Rather, they had agreed to simply meet at the sidelines while Hank cheered for his son, Nick at Pace Academy's athletic field. Nick was back in school and working out with the football team again.

While Stokes and Hank watched the scrimage, Bob gave Hank the news.

"It's his mom. She's the one. She lets him use her car, a red 2006 Dodge Charger. Kind'a strange for a woman of her age to be driving a muscle car, like she's the 'little old lady from Pasadena' or something."

"You going to give me the plate number"

"Relax. I've got it all on a memory stick. I'll give it to you when we shake hands, when we say goodbye in a few minutes."

"So there's more?"

"A lot more. He's got a guardian angel."

"What do you mean?"

"I mean, every time he gets into trouble, he somehow gets out of trouble. Be it financial difficulties or legal troubles, someone somehow intervenes in just the right way, and 'poof' the problem no longer exists.

"So who is it, his mother?"

"No, it's too big for a Walmart greeter like her. I don't know, but it's someone he's been associated with for a long time. Maybe even from when he served in the Army."

"Seiprecht served?"

"Yeah, I put a scan of his posting and deployment records on that stick."

"Did he have any special qualifications? What was his trade?"

"He was a prison guard or a military policeman or something. You're more qualified to go through his service records than I am. But nothing special, he was just a grunt, and he did not serve for very long," said Bob, suddenly smiling broadly.

"OK, Bob, give it up, what are you holding back?"

"The cabin."

Hank's heart leapt to his throat with hope. He could almost see himself breaking through the door and finding his daughter alive."

"Cabin?"

"Yeah. I almost missed it, because it wasn't in his mother's name at all. I had to go all the way back to records in Philadelphia, where his grandmother lives."

"Grandmother?"

"Yeah, she lives in an old folks home. The old lady is 88 years old and still as sharp as a tack."

"You met her?"

"Yup. I pretended to be a friend of his from the Army, trying to track him down. She told me that he lived in Rainbow Springs, which we know. So then I just let her go on talking, telling me her life story, just to see where it would take us."

"Give me the short version, Bob, I can't take the suspense."

Nick was losing his focus. He had already missed two important blocks and his QB had been sacked badly. But the presence of his father and that strange guy talking to him was really captivating his attention. He could tell from his Dad's body language that something important was going on.

"Coach, I need to sit out for a few plays, OK?"

"Sure, Carter. Take all the time you need, and give your head a shake. I don't have any more spare Quarterbacks. You gotta do your job right when you come back in, got it?"

"Yeah, coach. Thanks," said Nick as he turned and rushed off the field.

He was sure that his father wouldn't even notice.

Back on the sidelines, Bob Stokes was talking about Granny Seiprecht in Pennsylvania.

"You know, they were once a big deal in Pennsylvania, the Seibolds."

"I thought it was 'Seiprecht?'"

"Yes, it is. But some of the family used the South German spelling. And that's why we missed it at first. You see, old Grandpa was not that good with the

English, after getting off the boat back in 1920. Anyhow, the first thing he did was to buy up a mineral claim in what we now call –"

"The Nantahala forest!"

"Right."

"What sort of a claim was it?"

"It was a placer mine. Story goes, he panned for two years before he figured out it was more profitable to sell supplies to the other prospectors. Then he moved back to PA and built up the family business. Back in the day they were the largest outfitters in northern Pennsylvania. But then he died, in the sixties. The old woman has been living off the proceeds ever since."

"So is she David Seiprecht's sugar daddy?"

"No. Not directly. From what I could glean she sends David's mother an allowance of a few thousand dollars a month, but nothing directly to David because of his... pedigree."

"What?"

"He's a bastard."

"We know that."

"No, I mean *illegitimate*. And grandma has strong feelings about that."

"I'm confused. I thought she supported him and knew all about him. So you mean she did not want to acknowledge him, because he was illegitimate?"

"No, it's more complex than that. She loves the guy, but she has to play the game, pretending he does not exist so as to protect the reputation and in her words, the *heavenly soul* of her daughter. But she does care for her grandson. She even pretends that she knows nothing about his crimes."

"OK, I get the picture. She actually sounds like a nice old lady."

"Yeah. And she's so proud of her grandson for his army days with the Military Police."

"So tell me more about the cabin."

"Well, I've scanned in the title search and the plot plan – it's forty acres at the end of Silvermine, just a few miles outside of the declared search area, you know."

"I'm going out there tonight."

"Suit yourself, but I'm not going with you this time. And you'll probably get busted by the Sheriffs for violating that restraining order Seiprecht has against you."

"Understood. But thanks for developing all that info. Is there anything else?"

"Oh, I got a bunch of documents from the SBI and the Feds on their OPERATION NANNY. There's a really interesting set of notes on the FBI looking into the death of the Swain County Sheriff, and –"

"What? Sheriff Clarkson is dead? When did that happen?"

"You didn't hear? It happened the day he escorted you out of state – Don't worry, you're in the clear. Agent Dunwoody is on record that he picked you up at the state line, and monitored you all the way home. No. Sheriff Clarkson died accidentally in Macon County. "

"What was he doing there?"

"Hard to say. The FBI report suggests he was checking over some missing evidence from the search for the Harper girl, but the report from the senior investigator in the Macon County Sheriff's Department says he was just there on a friendly call to see his buddy, Sheriff Singer."

"Let me guess. That report was from Sergeant Fraser?"

"How'd you know?" Bob asked, looking at Hank in a new light. "Apparently Clarkson accidentally shot himself somehow in the Macon County Sheriff's Department."

"Yeah, right. Sounds kind of fishy to me!"

"Oh, you'd be surprised at how many accidental discharges LEOs have. Anyhow, it's all on the stick. And there are a few documents from the State and County guys up in Tennessee on the other subjects you gave me, but none of them look promising. I think you're right, this Seiprecht guy could be it." Bob paused, then looked at Hank as though for the last time. "And I mean this: Call the cops in as soon as you get a speck of solid evidence. Don't be stupid," he said, knowing with certainty that Hank would not listen to his advice.

"Get ready for that secret squirrel handshake. By the way, you do see that Agent Yeoman has a telephoto lens on us?"

"Does he? Oh, yeah, not too subtle, is he? But it's nice to know he's there if I need him. Let's do it, what do I do?"

"Just stand there." Bob moved in a small arc, standing face-to- face with Hank as he put his back to Agent Yeoman, blocking his camera angle. He reached out to grasp Hank's hand in a firm handshake, and then turned and left.

Hank closed his hand around the memory stick and then casually put his hand in his pants pocket, feeling like an experienced spy passing secrets in some kind of espionage novel.

But neither Hank nor Bob had noticed that Nick had been standing nearby, listening to their conversation. Nick had turned away just before the handshake and had already jogged onto the field to rotate back into the lineup before his father had even tried to get his mind back on his son's performance.

Nick played the rest of the scrimmage with surprising energy, drawing more than a few "hey, save it for the game!" comments.

17

CABIN

Now it was Nick's turn to play the spy. He knew that his father would be leaving, going after Seiprecht at the cabin, but he was not sure what to do. So he just did what he could to be prepared to act if needed. And then his father made it a little easier, and did the one thing that he had done so many times for Abby but had rarely done for Nick – he included Nick in his thoughts and plans.

"Nick, come in here, we need to talk."

"Sure thing, Dad."

"Nick. Did you see the man I was talking with at your game?"

"Yeah. Who was he?"

"His name is Bob Stokes, and he is a private detective. I hired him to help me find Abby, and tonight he told me where she might be."

Nick was so happy that his father had told him the truth, and brought him into his confidence. That one simple gesture seemed to instantly close the wide gap that had existed between them ever since Abby had come into their family, the golden haired baby instantly becoming Hank's favorite. Somehow having replaced Abby as Hank's object of affection made finding her that much more urgent to Nicky.

"I know all about it, Dad. The cabin in the Nantahala forest? I was standing right behind you! I heard it all."

Astonished, Hank paused to integrate the significance of what Nick had just revealed. "Wow. You *are* good, Nick!"

"So what's the plan, Dad?"

"The Plan? Well, I was going to do this on my own, but frankly, I could use your help."

"What can I do, Dad?" Nick said, excitedly.

"Here's what I need you to do…" he began.

Half an hour later, after the Carter men had finished preparing what they needed; the operation was put into motion.

Just as Yeoman was keying in his handover notes for Special Agent Dunwoody, who would be relieving half an hour later, the Carters' garage door opened and the minivan pulled out.

The agent noticed that Carter was in his military uniform, and presumed that he was headed to the base. At an obvious but not close distance, he followed the minivan towards Dobson Air Force Base.

As soon as the minivan and FBI shadow were clear, Mrs. Carter's car pulled out of the driveway and was soon heading eastbound on Village Parkway.

Fifteen minutes later, Hank took off the ridiculous wig he had improvised out of a Halloween witch costume, just in case someone had been watching. Marjorie herself was still asleep, one of the side effects of the medication that the great Dr. Peel had increasingly hooked her on. She had not been brought in on the plan.

Nick was a little afraid when he approached the Air Force base dressed in his father's uniform, but there was no actual danger. Had he tried to enter the base, his deception would most certainly have been detected by the sentries at the gate. But as he was driving right past the south entrance and continuing to the Post Exchange, the PX, on the north side of the base, in the non-secure area accessible to the general public, there was little risk of detection.

Nick worried about was being pulled over by a traffic cop or a military policeman, because at the ripe old age of fifteen, he did not have a license to drive. As it was, he had pretty good driving skills thanks to the lessons his father had given him on dirt roads whenever they went camping or on the occasional visit to Grandma and Grandpa Carter's home in rural Minnesota.

To keep the deception from coming apart, Nick had to actually get out of the minivan and enter the PX.

Agent Yeoman had seen Hank do this many times before. According to the psych profiler working with the FBI, Captain Carter was still not ready to return to work, and was following the psychiatrist's prescription that he gradually adjust to it by making small trips to the base for little tasks, in uniform, to establish the rhythm of a normal work routine.

Only in this case, it was Hank's fifteen year old son who went into the PX to buy a chocolate bar.

It had almost worked. But due to the physical mismatch between Hank and Nick, the uniform looked baggy and strange on him. One of the other shoppers, a Military Police sergeant, had picked up on the details while Nick was inside the PX. He did not confront Nick, as he was trained in counter-FOIS -Foreign Operational Intelligence Surveillance – and knew that it was essential not to tip off a subject under surveillance. And judging by the small size and young appearance of the Caucasian boy impersonating an Air Force officer, the sergeant did not feel that there was any danger.

"Excuse me," he said to Nick, smiling at the terrified boy as he reached past him to grab a cigarette lighter from a display on a rack next to Nick. This gave the MP the chance to take a good look at the face and at the nametag on the boys' ill-fitting uniform.

"Captain," said the MP sergeant, tipping his hat.

With his heart pounding in his chest, Nick stuffed the change into his pocket, and walked quickly out to the parking lot.

The MP did not follow, he simply noted the plate on the rear of the vehicle and called in the Sight-Rep.

Parked at the far end of the parking lot from the Carter minivan, the newly promoted Special Agent Yeoman was a still a step behind his assignment. He had not registered the MP's counter-surveillance on Nick, and he had still had not picked up on it by the time Nick climbed into the vehicle.

Before Nick had even left the parking lot, the MP had been told not to follow the minivan, that local law enforcement would be informed, and that there was an open file on Captain Carter, flagged "Refer all reports to FBI point of contact."

At the same time Nick pulled the vehicle back into the garage at home, Special Agent Yeoman was informed that he had been hoodwinked yet again, and had lost his assignment. Yeoman was shocked and distressed to learn that he had been following a decoy.

Meanwhile, Hank had already passed Clayton, GA and would be in North Carolina within minutes.

Hank had ceased worrying about whether the Feds or the County Sheriff's boys would be watching for Marjorie's station wagon. If they tried to pull him over, Hank thought, he would just keep going as he had done with the sea container, and guide them to Granny Seiprecht's cabin. As it was, he hoped the boring appearance of the somewhat dated, typically suburban Buick station-wagon would not be noticed on the busy highway.

But there were no flashing lights in his rear-view mirror, and the occasional Sheriff's Deputy he saw along the way did not look at him twice.

That was it! Hank thought to himself as he slowed the station-wagon, looking for a place to turn around or pull in to park.

When he left Atlanta, Hank thought about approaching from the south by taking Winding Stairs Road and then roughing the dirt tracks that linked the start of Fairview Lane with the end of Silvermine Road, but then decided it was too risky. He could just as easily get mired in muck or lost in un-marked roads in the hills.

The driveway to the cabin was near the end of Silvermine Road. A hand-made sign identified the driveway. Hank read the old sign mounted on a tree, 'SEIBOLD'. His heart raced, as his adrenal glands kicked into overdrive. He was instantly pumped for danger.

247

Hank continued on and finally pulled into the next dirt track that led to the left, off Silvermine Road.

He looked around as he drove slowly along the track. From the stumps and wood chips around, Hank figured he was in someone's woodlot. The track soon ended in a rough clearing, where 4x4s had made a rutted mess of the ground.

He drove carefully, to turn the station wagon around without getting stuck in the ruts, and then shut off the engine. He got out and looked carefully at his surroundings. There was no sign of anybody.

Good, thought Hank, *I'll have surprise on my side.*

Taking his wooden baseball bat from the trunk of the Buick,, Hank set off through the woods, back towards the Seibold property. It did not take long. The terrain was mature re-growth poplar forest, with thick tree-trunks and only thin underbrush underneath.

When he got to the edge of a large clearing, with the small cabin visible on the opposite side, he became tensely coiled, like a hunter, and held his trusty baseball bat that much tighter. His bat had smacked more than a few balls in its day, but in this inning it was reserved for smacking skulls.

A red muscle car with the same plate number that Bob Stokes had provided, was parked close by. For the first time, Hank was certain that he had him, and was about to move in for the kill. He decided it was too risky to cross the open field, so he worked his way around to the east, staying just inside the forest as he circled counter-clockwise around the clearing.

Suddenly Hank heard a twig snap behind him. He turned around, expecting to see a shotgun aimed at his face, and saw a five foot tall buck with a six-point rack, just ten yards away. The animal looked alertly at Hank, and then loped away into the forest.

Hank fought to resume his normal breathing, and carried on to the backside of the cabin, where it was closer to the tree line.

All of the windows in the cabin were covered with tin foil. The cabin itself was made of logs. Hank crept up to the rear window of the cabin, next to a narrow chimney made of small river rocks and mortar.

He raised himself up, listening for sounds from inside. As his head reached the bottom of the window, he looked for any gaps or seams in the tin foil, and found none.

He went around to a side window, where he saw a small gap in the foil at the bottom right hand corner of a window. Peering in, Hank could not make out much at first, as it was much darker inside the cabin. He worried for a moment that he might be noticed, but as his one eye grew accustomed to the dark, he saw Seiprecht standing next to a bed in the far corner of the cabin. Hank could make out a figure lying on the bed, but could not see the facial features, hidden from his view in an alcove.

Gripping his bat firmly, Hank decided to mount his attack from the front of the cabin.. He rounded the corner, and began creeping across to the door at the far end of the front wall. His left boot caught an unseen and mostly buried rock. Hank stumbled. The noise was almost imperceptible but the ensuing quiet was unbearable. Then the magnitude of his sudden predicament hit Hank like a jack-hammer - HOLY SHIT!

"Who's out there?" called a voice from inside.

Hank froze for a moment, and considered running for self-preservation. He had a quick mental image of himself eating a shotgun, cowered down by the chimney at the back.

Fuck that, he thought as he rushed the front door, arriving just as it was yanked open.

He saw the shotgun rising to his face before he even saw the goatee on David Seiprecht's chin.

18

DELIVERANCE

Special Agent Yeoman did not stand around waiting for Dunwoody and the others to arrive at the Carter residence. He had royally screwed up, again. He could remember the words of Special Agent-in-Charge, Dunbar, when he had begrudgingly granted Yeoman his upgrade from Probationary to full Special Agent. It had come with a warning: "One more screw up, Special Agent Yeoman, and you'll not only lose your promotion, but you'll also be given a written reprimand. You know what that means?" Dunbar had asked, rhetorically. "That means you will be one short step away from dismissal from the Bureau."

In Daryl Yeoman's mind, he had only one choice. To track down Carter before the other agents did, and hopefully save his career in the process.

From inside the house, Nick saw the FBI agent he had spoofed so brilliantly suddenly drive off like a bat out of hell!

Nick knew where Agent Yeoman was headed. Yeoman had really pressed Nick hard about why he and his dad had gone to such great lengths to deceive him. Yeoman seemed genuinely terrified for Hank's safety, so Nick had told him what he knew of his father's destination.

Nick hoped that the FBI would arrive in time to back his father up. But something about Agent Yeoman made Nick worry that only the single agent would go to his father's rescue, probably with a holstered Glock. The cavalry used horses and swords in the old days. Nicky Carter decided to ride to his father's side. His imagination took hold as the garage door opened. He got his breathing under control, programmed the GPS to Silvermine Road, and finally put the limited horsepower on the road. Captain Henry Carter of the USAF had taught his son well.

The hollow sound of the baseball bat clashing with the barrel of the shotgun marked the start of the battle.

David Seiprecht had been surprised to see Hank Carter at his doorstep. Hank's greater mass and momentum had carried the two men through the doorway and into the cabin. Sensing that his opponent was off balance, Hank worked his feet like a linebacker as he shoved the bat firmly into Seiprecht's neck and arm, forcing the shotgun over his right shoulder.

David swore as his fingers were twisted off the handgrip and the shotgun fell to the floor. He was suddenly pressed up against the cabin wall, with Hank leaning into him as if he wanted to smear him into the rough logs of the wall behind him. David kneed Hank, catching him high in the thigh. It was enough to push Hank off balance, and presented an opening. He spun around, causing Hank to smash into the cabin wall. Then he grabbed hold of Hank's left hand and used a submission technique he had learned as a military policeman.

Hank let out a scream as his fingers were forced backwards and his arm was twisted awkwardly behind him. The shot of pain was intense, and his right hand opened. The baseball bat obeyed the laws of gravity.

"You piece of shit! How the hell did you find me? No matter, it'll just add to the show when I blow your fucking head off!" screamed the degenerate pervert into Hank's right ear, as he forced the bigger man down.

David released his grip at the explosion of the shotgun. Despite the pain, Hank had desperately snatched the shotgun from the floor with his right hand and inadvertently pulled the trigger.

As the BOOM resonated in the confined space, David jerked backwards as Hank fell on his ass against the end of the bed. Carter raised his new-found weapon directly at the object of his murderous obsession. He re-cocked the shotgun.

"Hold on. Not so fast. There's no need for this," pleaded David Seiprecht, thinking of what he could possibly grab and throw at the man who now had the bead on him.

Hank looked at the girl on the bed. He noticed that she had dark hair, not the blond hair of his daughter.

"Where's my daughter? What have you done to her!" thundered the voice of Captain Henry Carter as he rose slowly and attained his impressive stature.

"Your little bitch? I almost had her, by the river, after I already had this cunt. But you know what? She threw a rock at my van or something, and ran away!"

"You're lying! What did you do to her?"

"Hey, no fuckin' shit! I missed her. I wish I had her! We wanted two girls for the show, but before I could grab her, she fell in the river. You pathetic prick. The last sight I had of her was her scrawny body heading down to Patton's Run, floating like a bloated, yellow turd in the river."

Seiprecht was now leaning on the countertop that made up the little kitchen on the front wall of the cabin, with his hands gripping the edge of the counter. Hank looked beyond him, checking for knives or pots that could be used as weapons.

"What have you done to this girl? Is she alive?"

"Oh yeah, she's alive. She's just in la-la land right now. She's come to like the type of candy I've been giving her. She put up quite a fight the first few times."

Hank looked at the girl again. She was breathing regularly, like a child does when sleeping. Her hands were chained to the ironwork of the headboard, her legs unbound. The messed up hair, the bruises on her face and body, and the fact that she was completely naked made it abundantly clear to Hank Carter that she had been repeatedly sexually assaulted by this degenerate excuse for a human being.

Hank was just opening his mouth to say something when he saw a whirl coming towards him. He jerked back out of reflex, squeezing the trigger involuntarily.

BOOM! The shotgun went off again, instantly flooding the cabin with bright sunlight as the window behind Hank's adversary blew apart.

The whirl was a plate of utensils. They smashed into Hank's face. He was momentarily blinded and did not see the round-house kick coming at him. It connected with his head, giving his eyes a sharp flash of black-and-white cubes as an afterimage, his brain reporting the solid jolt on his skull. Hank had a fleeting sensation of spinning as his knees buckled under him, his hands let go of the shotgun, and he collapsed in a heap.

David Seiprecht hesitated for only a second, hopped up and down as he recovered from the first kick, and then proceeded to set himself up for another blow. He then weighed the efficacy of the shotgun against a fist-strike to the head.

"Freeze asshole!" commanded Yeoman."FBI!"

David Seiprecht froze for only an instant.

David dove for the shotgun, grabbed it, and continued in a forward role as Yeoman fired, striking Seiprecht a glancing blow on his shoulder, the bullet burning a track through his denim shirt and drawing only a little blood.

As he tracked the tumbling Seiprecht with his Glock, Daryl Yeoman regretted not having called for backup. He had caught up to Hank only to become stuck in the dirt track. He had been unable to pick up any trail when he reached Hank's car.

Yeoman had no idea where Hank had gone, but when he heard the first shotgun blast, his desperation to salvage his assignment propelled him across the clearing without taking the time to assess the situation.

Had he been more thorough when he had lost Hank that day in Franklin, Yeoman might have learned of the transcripts Hank acquired at the courthouse, and understood more about Hank's obsession with tracking down David Seiprecht.

As it was, he had thought that Hank's visit to the Macon County Sheriff's office had something to do with one of the staff there. Agent Yeoman had quickly interviewed Deputy Martin, who had told him that Hank had taken away a copy of the org-chart, with the pictures of the Macon County Sheriff's personnel. Daryl had assumed that Hank's entire trip to Franklin had something to do with Carter's ongoing troubles with law enforcement, perhaps an attempt to gather information on Sergeant Fraser, who was known to be antagonistic towards Captain Carter.

Had he been more thorough, Yeoman might have picked up on Hank's interest in the registered sex offender registry, and in the history of David Seiprecht – potentially a murderous sociopath.

As it was, he only figured out the latter when he became aware of the girl trussed out on the bed, the outstretched arms of Hank trying to reach Seiprecht, and the muzzle of the shotgun coming to bear on his own chest. The sound of his impending doom was the re-cocking of a shotgun.

The dazzling light from the muzzle was the last thing that Special Agent Yeoman ever comprehended.

The expanding blast of shotgun pellets ripped through Yeoman's rib cage, ravaging the fragile bones, tearing his heart to shreds and blowing through his spine. The exit wound from the blast was almost ten inches wide.

He was dead before he hit the ground.

Seiprecht awkwardly re-cocked the shotgun once again. Hank's hands were now closing around his throat, squeezing off his air supply.

With his veins swelling and his face turning beet red, David pushed the muzzle against Hank's belly and pulled the trigger.

There was no report. The shotgun was empty.

He was beginning to black out as the oxygen in his brain depleted. Hank was now leaning hard onto his prey, adding the force of his weight and the push of his legs to the grip his hands had on the murderer's neck.

The jolt of the steel pipe striking his chin was like an electric shock to Carter's brain, snapping his head back like a boxer getting hit with a vicious uppercut.

He let go of his hold.

David gasped for air and then struck Hank repeatedly with the hollow end of the shotgun muzzle, quickly moving out of reach as if Hank's hands themselves where his enemy.

Having regained freedom and dominance over his assailant, Seiprecht once again tried to cocked and fire the shotgun, only to have the same empty result. He flashed on the memory that he had only had three shells in it.

So he turned the weapon around. First hitting Hank's hands and arms, which were raised in a defensive manner, the pedophile used the hard-wooden butt of the shotgun like a club.

Hank tried to raise his hands again, but this time the best effort he could muster was to waive them feebly as his head was repetitiously battered by the wood.

Rewarded for his efforts by the sight of blood gushing and splashing from Hank's head, David stopped to admire his handiwork.

Catching his breath and feeling the rush of deliverance from the unexpected attack, he basked in the glory of defeating not one, but two potential adversaries.

"Who the fuck do you think you are? Coming into a man's home and assaulting him!"

Seiprecht said this as he laid a heavy kick into Hank's ribs. He felt more than heard bones cracking in Hanks chest. Carter was out cold, the centerpiece of a seemingly unstoppable and expanding pool of blood.

David looked over his shoulder to see if the action had been caught in the pan of the camera on the table, connected to his computer for the live broadcast he had barely started when he was interrupted by the sound of Hank approaching the domain of his debauchery.

"You get that, buddy?" he questioned the other end of the Internet link, as his every movement was captured in the live feed. With no audio link, he did not expect an answer. David saw the red light on the camera and the moving icon on the laptop indicating transmission, so he figured he was still live.

Hank and the dead agent were in full view of the camera, in the foreground of the main feature laid out on the bed. He positioned himself at right angles, so that he would be in profile view as he delivered the killing blow to the defenseless man at his feet.

As he thought about watching his performance later, in a safe place, his train of thought put the killing blow on pause. Suddenly worried that there could be teams of agents moving in to surround the cabin, he was compelled to look outside for any signs of activity.

Expecting to see agents moving into his doorway in tactical formation, he put the empty shotgun down and picked up the baseball bat – *much more suitable for close-combat,* he thought, as he stepped carefully out the door.

19

END TO ANGUISH

Relishing the death blow he would soon go back in to deliver to Hank Carter, David Seiprecht stood a few yards outside of the cabin.

He listened for the normal sounds of the forest he knew so well, recognizing immediately that something was wrong. As he tuned his hearing, he heard something in the distance.

He was surprised that there were no additional cars parked near the cabin. He began to wonder where that asshole with the bat had come from and where the FBI agent's cruiser was parked. Wherever it was, there could be more out there.

He walked out a bit farther, brandishing Carter's baseball bat, searching for a possible adversary. "Bring it to me, assholes. I don't give a flyin' fuck who you are. I'll beat you to a pulp, and when I'm done with you, I'll drink your fuckin' blood !" he ranted.

Hank opened his eyes, with a headache the size of Lake Michigan. As he tried to bring the bright and blurry picture in front of him into focus he began to register the injuries to his head, his ribs, and his legs. An upwelling anguish assailed his heart at the disappointment of not finding Abby, his beloved lost child.

The rising pain brought him greater awareness. He could smell the coppery metallic stench of the pool of blood his cheek was resting in, and he could also sense the unusual smell of what? Almonds?

As his vision improved, Hank realized that he couldn't move, and that he was on the floor. He had been winning the fight. *What went wrong?* Then he saw the dancing blur in the brightness, through the doorframe. Seiprecht was standing there, holding Hank's bat in his left hand, muttering to himself or to someone Hank could not see.

And then Hank realized that he had blown it. He should have called the Feds. But he hadn't. He made out the agent lying nearby, dead on the floor, and knew that he was responsible for his death.

The realization that the girl he had been about to rescue was not his daughter flooded through him. Then he remembered something Seiprecht had said, that Abby had gotten away, floating down the river like a 'bloated yellow turd.'

Hank was getting dizzy, slipping back into unconsciousness. But then he realized, with a slight sliver of hope, that Seiprecht may have been telling the truth, that he had not abducted Abby, only the Harper girl who must surely be the one on the bed. *He didn't get Abby!*

Then he heard a familiar, odd, clicking sound as a vehicle pulled into the area in front of the cabin.

Our minivan… Oh shit! Nicky!

Hank tried to move, but couldn't budge.

He tried to call out to warn Nick, but could only manage a hoarse gasp.

As his cone of vision closed in on him, with his last vestige of consciousness, Hank recognized the Carter family minivan approaching through the trees before disappearing behind the cabin and out of his view. He heard his fifteen-year old son open the door, and then saw Seiprecht moving stealthily around the corner with the bat in his hand. He looked predatory.

With his body battered and his consciousness slipping away, Hank was no match for what then replaced his physical pain. A hellish new level of anguish assailed him to the core.

His last thought before passing out was that his obsession with hunting Seiprecht, his futile months of self-pity and wasted energy, had led his son to a lonely death and had done nothing at all to help Abby.

He had failed them both, terribly, and would die a pitiful fool.

The End

The next book in the series, *Lost Child (Vol II) – Retribution in the Nantahala* by Gene Skellig, is available at Amaon.com or www.fleacircusbooks.com
For paperback, go to www.createspace.com/3884845
Enter Code: H8FCEL7U for a **$3.00 discount.**

Check out other Flea Circus books:

Winter Kill – *War With China Has Already Begun:* by Gene Skellig. www.createspace.com/3537111 Enter Code PAC6SETA for $3.50 off

Homestay – *A Japanese Girl's Romantic ESL Adventure In Vancouver,* Canada: by Gene Skellig www.createspace.com/ 3715916 Enter Code 9JGPMV3B for $2.50 off.

Health Quest – *Fantasize Yourself to a Hard Body* www.createspace.com/3625224

Altered – *Revelations of the Evolved*, by Shawnda Currie. www.createspace.com/3882371 Enter Code: F7UA8S7H for $2.00 off.

For additional discount codes and undiscovered authors visit: www.fleacircusbooks.com

ABOUT THE AUTHOR

Currently serving as an Air Force pilot, Gene was inspired to write *Lost Child* by a very clever nine year old girl. About to retire from the Air Force, Gene plans to transition to a semi-retired lifestyle of writing and publishing books and enjoying the Vancouver Island lifestyle. Gene has studied an eclectic range of subjects, and has a degree in Philosophy from the University of British Columbia in his home town of Vancouver. Gene is also a founding member of Flea Circus Books. To find out more about Gene, explore his page through FleaCircusBooks.com or the Gene Skellig author page at Amazon.com.